# A HISTORY OF TOMLINSON HALL

BY

HULTA GERTRUDE

Copyright © HULTA GERTRUDE 2024
This book is sold subject to the condition that it shall not, by way of trade or otherwise, be lent, resold, hired out, or otherwise circulated without the publisher's prior consent in any form of binding or cover other than that in which it is published and without a similar condition including this condition being imposed on the subsequent publisher.
The moral right of HULTA GERTRUDE has been asserted.
ISBN-13: 9798877945401

This is a work of fiction. Names, characters, businesses, organizations, places, events and incidents either are the product of the author's imagination or are used fictitiously. Any resemblance to actual persons, living or dead, events, or locales is entirely coincidental.

*This work is dedicated to the memory of Polly-Ann Smyth (1948-2022), without whom this book simply couldn't exist.*

*Rest in peace Kat, go easy on those heavenly tequilas, and may the summer of 1970 never end for you.*

# Foreword

The truth is, I wanted to give a preface to this work. However, as I'm unable to tell if what I've read is fictional or not, I decided on a foreword instead. In my long career as a bus driver, and after a lifetime of underachievement and blundering endeavours, I've found that the past is made up of a few facts and a lot of opinions. In my opinion, this book, if indeed one can call it that, couldn't have been any worse than what I'd been reading before. So, I was shocked at the mysterious and compelling nature of the content. Frankly, almost as astounded as my passengers. I would recommend it to all fans of literature, and it has certainly made my first few weeks in jail much easier to bear. Best wishes to the author … whoever they are.

*Alexander Kemp*

*"Never before have I encountered such a potent spiritual divide."*
Maria Hayden, 1853

*"Home sweet home, where the hearts are, where it is good to be."*
Tomlinson Hall, stained-glass inscription

# CONTENTS

FOREWORD ................................................................................................. i
PROLOGUE ................................................................................................. 1
CHAPTER 1: *The Codicil* .......................................................................... 2
CHAPTER 2: *Forgettable for All the Right Reasons* ............................... 14
CHAPTER 3: *The Twin Fates of Primrose* ............................................. 19
CHAPTER 4: *Tomlinson Hall: Part One: We Are All Made of Dust* ..... 31
CHAPTER 5: *Dear Darkest Solitude: Unawake* ..................................... 44
CHAPTER 6: *Dear Darkest Solitude: Sleepless* ...................................... 57
CHAPTER 7: *I, Jack Tomlinson, a Resident of Albany-on-Lea ...* ........ 82
CHAPTER 8: *A Church, a Pub and a School* ......................................... 96
CHAPTER 9: *Tomlinson Hall: Part Two: Only Open Eyes Can See* .... 110
CHAPTER 10: *What about us?* ............................................................. 123
CHAPTER 11: *Whispers from the Dead* ............................................... 136
CHAPTER 12: *The Past, the Treasures and the Reckoning* ................. 149
CHAPTER 13: *Tomlinson Hall: Part Three: Home* .............................. 159
CHAPTER 14: *Primrose would have been proud* ................................ 170
CHAPTER 15: *The Ninth from 1970* .................................................... 181
EPILOGUE ............................................................................................... 184
AFTERWORD .......................................................................................... 186
APPENDICES .......................................................................................... 187

# PROLOGUE

As Robin stared into the hole in the ground, he couldn't help but wonder what was all this for? Father had said that someone once very dear to him would never return, and Mother had told him something he didn't understand about ashes and dust. The huge raindrops, coming down from the grey sky and the lips of black umbrellas, were turning the mud into a pond. Robin could hear the tapping sound that the water made on the coffin, while a man in white said many words to the crowd. Old Primrose was gone, never to return, but it was what he'd left behind that would make the largest impression on Robin.

# CHAPTER ONE

## The Codicil

It was too late: the bedroom door was open, and all the desperate pretences shattered.

He'd heard the post land on the mat, and despite repeated shouts of 'sit' and 'no', Fido was on the loose! All of this was why thirty-three kilos of overly friendly German Shepherd was hurtling towards the front door at a terrifying velocity. Olivia had done her best, flinging herself across the bed dramatically in a futile effort to prevent the inevitable. Her fingertips had just brushed his tail, far too late to grab his collar, and she was the athletic one. Indeed, part of the whole reason for getting Fido in the first place was to make her jogging experiences safer.

Robin had been halfway through shaving, and still had the cutthroat pressed against his skin when it had happened. It took all his self-discipline not to cut himself as he tried to stop the dog by shouting. He was saving up for an electric razor on the side, but it had been slow work.

"Fido, stay!" implored Olivia over the barking. "No! Come here!" She ran down the hallway and halted as she surveyed the damage. Fido was sitting there, panting, tongue lolling out, drool flowing, looking all innocent and happy as always.

"What's he done now?" called Robin, with a forlorn sigh. Olivia pushed her glasses further up her nose as she crouched by the ruins. The newspaper was gone – just gone. Nothing was left, there was no use even looking at this point, they knew it would never be seen again. Not all bad news then, some might say. A few takeaway leaflets had been badly mauled too, but one of them was still recognisable. Incredibly, a lone letter remained and had apparently escaped the chaos unmolested. Fido must be slipping …

"You bad boy, Fido!" she scolded with a groan. He barked and started licking her face, making her push him away.

His face still decorated with outcroppings of shaving cream, Robin finally caught up.

"I think we need to get that gate …" she said, referring to a discussion they'd had earlier in the week.

"There's no point, he'll jump over it, and we can't afford the big one," he argued levelly.

"He's already getting too big for me to stop," she said, looking up at him pleadingly. Robin beheld his girlfriend standing before him, Fido next to her. When on his hind legs, Fido was as tall as she was. As a puppy, he'd been so cute and controllable. Frighteningly, at eleven months and four days, he'd not even finished growing yet! While he didn't like to admit it, maybe they'd made a booboo.

"Look, it doesn't matter now," she sighed, hugging him. "You've got to go, or you'll be late."

"Yes," Robin agreed as she rubbed the last of the shaving cream off his face. He made a dash for the door after she tried to make his tie look like a human had done it up.

"Case!" she yelled at him. He stopped and spun around a few times before grabbing his briefcase and jacket.

"Love you!" he declared as he threw himself out of the door.

"Love you!" she shouted back. She stared back at Fido who was by now used to the idea that his master had to go some places without him.

"Can you please stop eating our mail, Fido?" she pleaded, not being serious. She knew, despite him clearly understanding every word spoken in plain English, there was no way he'd oblige. That was when she picked up the surviving letter. She knew she had to log-on in an hour but that left plenty of time for breakfast and all manner of other essential activities. She was lucky she worked from home. Granted, it didn't pay as much as some other positions, but the expediency was not to be sneezed at. With Fido brushing against her all the way, she entered the kitchen to refill his water and food – even if he had just eaten. While he acted like he'd not just feasted on their correspondence by diving in like a starving animal, Olivia sat at the table. After putting the microwave on, she brushed her sleep-tousled hair away from her eyes, pushed her glasses back up her nose, and opened the letter.

The microwave pinged; she didn't look up or acknowledge it at all, so engrossed was she in the letter. Fido finished his meal, sat beside her and stared up patiently. She slowly placed the letter on the table and stared down into his big brown eyes with her grey ones. He tilted his head to one side and gave a tiny high-pitched whine, making him unbearably cute.

"Okay," she murmured slowly. Olivia believed in perseverance, but she knew when she needed help and had no problems asking for it. She texted Robin, letting him know that she had some interesting news for him but that she needed him to see if his dad would be around that evening as they would most likely need his help.

Little did she realise, at that instant, events that transpired later in the day would muddle an already intricate situation.

*

There are some words that have negative connotations, inescapable implications, which only the very young or very innocent might miss. Discrimination, for example, or practically anything that ends in an -ism. Racism, ageism ... antidisestablishmentarianism. Many of these are subjective and dictated by the opinions and emotions of individuals at any given point in time. As Barry Mandela said, 'Words are the most dangerous weapons of all' and, certainly in these times, he would be right.

The words in question on this occasion are: transformation, voluntary redundancy (two for one there), hiatus, imminent, and management. A whole page of connotations could be detailed on each one of those terms. No doubt most people would be able to write those pages themselves. Such phrases are infamous enough to have reached the majority of people in one form or another. Imagine the horror it would cause were you to hear all these words within the same presentation. That was the dismay that Robin was going through at that moment.

*Side note: 'imminent' may seem the odd one out in the selection above; however, natural disasters, when soon to begin, are often described as imminent.*

Robin was sitting in an office surrounded by colleagues who, despite their physical diversity, looked eerily alike – particularly at that moment. Wide-eyed, tense, silent and attentive, they all watched as the company director explained their potential future to them. Despite knowing he should listen to every word – his career depended on it – Robin couldn't stop his mind wandering. Olivia didn't get paid enough to deal with the rent and the bills on her own and, even if she did, he'd never put her in that position. They had literally no savings as they'd spent it all on Fido and a new laptop (a laptop needed for work).

What kind of sick, depraved, devil-worshipping company makes its employees buy their own laptops? Alas, these days, it was all too common. The 'job for life' was gone, the property market had turned into the VIP's entrance at the nightclub (you know, the one you're not allowed to use), and on top of everything else, Robin felt that his generation was at once being blamed for everything that went wrong while also having to suffer from the consequences of past mistakes. It wasn't fair, the child in his mind screamed as it burst into make-believe tears. *Oh, woe, sadness, and grief, why do you test us?*

Forcing himself to concentrate again, he squared his shoulders, took a deep breath, and remembered Primrose's words: *don't let them get you down.*

He was being told how, due to unforeseen market fluctuations (corporate clairvoyance cock-up), they were looking to lay off 70% of staff within the next financial period. At last, this crushing revelation brought the crowd to life. There is no group expression for mass muttering, not that he could think of, so Robin decided to invent one. An utterance of muttering? Perhaps a standing of mutterings? A *murble* of mutterings? As his mind wandered, as it invariably did, it returned to Primrose and the funeral all those years ago.

He'd learned a lot about action and consequence at that time in his life. He'd not done anything wrong himself, but he'd been perceptive enough to pick up on a lot of the things other children may have missed, like what happened to people around someone who dies. The emotional, economic and, sometimes, just practical implications. He reflected that this presentation, while obviously not directly responsible for what they were all about to go through, would be a pivotal moment within it.

He had thought about Olivia first and, as he glanced around, he wondered how many hundreds of people would feel the knock-on effects. Families destroyed? Homes lost? Hopes kaput? Losing a job was a real and near-primal fear that lived in the consciousness of pretty much everyone who'd ever had one. Made manifest before him, he observed as his colleagues displayed it in one way or another. Olivia had, on occasion, insisted he could have become a psychologist as he spent a lot of time watching people and analysing their behaviour. Now, he saw a lot of shocked and dumbfounded expressions, as well as some thunderous ones among them.

One face stood out among the rest: that of Arni. Arnold Fernsby was sixteen years older than Robin, but he had become a close friend. He'd been the one to train Robin when he first joined and, while never managing him directly, he remained a constant on Robin's periphery. Tall, cadaverously thin, and in possession of a dark brown bowl-type haircut, Arni glared at the screen before them. Folding his arms, he made his ill-fitting tweed jacket ride up towards the back of his neck. The question was, would he remain stoically silent or launch into some scathingly apoplectic interrogation?

He had to be taking it personally about not having been informed prior to this, Robin supposed. As if detecting Robin's scrutiny, Arni made eye contact with him. He pulled a face and then made a drinking gesture with his undernourished hand. While Robin knew he had to get home and tell Olivia what had happened, Arni might be worth delaying his return for. Rarely did Arni miss a trick and he knew more about employment, work and the economy in general than Robin did. The guy had shares, pensions and contacts everywhere! Actual real investments and stuff on the side.

In all self-deprecating honesty, the only stake Robin had ever held was at a dinner party. In this situation, Arni could be a valuable connection to have in his network.

It wasn't as if Robin was looking forward to delivering the news, anyway. Hoping Olivia wouldn't be upset, Robin gave him an obvious nod of acceptance. Being cooped up in the house all day, with only the dog for company, she had occasionally expressed disappointment with him when he'd stayed out later than normal. He sent her a message to tell her he was going to be late, to at least give her some warning, but didn't check for a reply.

*

"Idiots! Absolute hypocritical two-faced idiots!" Arni was ranting. "No wonder they didn't want me in that meeting a few weeks ago! I knew they were up to something, and I could have done something about it but instead they chose to keep me in a state of endarkenment!" These weren't his exact words but, in these delicate times, Robin chose to switch a few around to lessen the blow. F-bombs were dropped aplenty, and their mushroom clouds of vulgar abuse would make even a veteran trooper raise an eyebrow.

"They don't practise what they preach, either …"

Only the hopping hipster beer finally brought silence to their table. Robin was closest to the door, nursing his half pint patiently – he didn't want to be there any longer than he had to. Arni and Erica (she'd come along for the ride) were glaring at each other across the table, both infuriated with the situation.

"I knew this was going to happen!" she declared, in that angry way people do. She hadn't really known anything. None of them had. Arni, the only one who might have heard something, seemed to have been purposely excluded.

"They knew I'd warn people," he went on, starting to calm down. A second pause in the conversation occurred as they seemed to sigh and relax a little as a trio. Erica worked in Human Resources, and apparently she had also been omitted from any relevant discussions. So she maintained, anyway … Robin wasn't quite sure he believed her, but it could be true.

"What do you think's going to happen next?" asked Robin, not knowing what to expect in terms of their answers.

"The Union will do nothing," Erica answered, rummaging in her handbag for something. "They'll give a few token blusters, no doubt, maybe indulge the farce of consultation, but nothing of any significance will they achieve."

"The managers, turns out, have been looking for other positions for weeks," muttered Arni, grimly.

"Why didn't any of them say something?" groaned Erica through her teeth.

"Now that I think back to the other day, I'm pretty sure one of them tried to. Neil and I exchanged a few remarks on my way out. He said something about moving on and updating his CV … at the time I didn't think much of it."

"I've not looked at mine for over a year," Erica said, as if stricken by anxiety. Robin had managed to keep his up to date but only because of Olivia's pestering. Never had the words *you never know what's never going to happen* been more significant. As one door opens, be sure to walk through and never mind who might not be there.

"Robin!" shouted Erica, knocking on the table as if declaring she was one card away from winning. He leapt free of the reverie he'd slipped into, soaring back into reality with well-practised ease.

"Yes?" he said, taking a slurp.

"What are you going to do?" she enquired, clearly not for the first time. Robin looked back and forth between them before shrugging.

"Go home and tell my girlfriend," he grunted.

\*

Wasn't it always the way that when you wanted a journey to drag on, the time just slipped by with unrivalled smoothness? Robin's commute typically could be described as an ordeal, the sort of thing that had to be suffered through, that sort of thing. Endured like a true test of tolerance and patience, even the peace-loving guinea pigs frequently turned violent. That evening, however, it was bucking the trend and Robin just wasn't feeling it.

He had discovered Olivia's text to him, telling him she had some interesting news, and, in his current frame of mind, that didn't make him feel any better. This was the woman who'd once described a house fire as a bit of a pickle – the mistress of understatement herself. Interesting news could mean anything from death and anarchy to a boiler malfunction. Perhaps her spot was back ... she hated that thing and refused to talk about it directly. She felt like an unwanted ghost, that talking about it or even just acknowledging its presence only served to encourage it.

How was he going to tell her that he would soon be out of a job? He needed more time to think it through – the last thing he wanted to do was get her worried.

He knew he had to tell her as she always somehow knew when he wasn't telling her things. He would go silent; she would think she'd done something wrong and start digging. This would cause increased frustration and even arguments, so he knew he had to tell her, if only to at least let her know that if he was silent or morose it wasn't because of her. That being said, how could he tell her that he might only have one last month's worth of money coming in without it triggering some level of anxiety?

He hurried down the street and started to chastise himself for being so self-absorbed. Olivia might already be worried, and he was dawdling when he could be being supportive. An explosion of excited barking broke out announcing his arrival before he got to the door. He struggled through into the hallway before being pinned to the wall and having his face licked off by Fido. It seemed a little redundant to proclaim his arrival as everyone on their street would have figured it out.

"Yes, I love you too!" he pleaded, fending off Fido's enthusiastic advances. "Sit! Sit!"

Olivia sprang from the nearest doorway, brandishing Fido's lead.

"Hi," she smiled, rising onto her toes to kiss him. He offered her the only portion of slobber-free face he had and put his arm around her. Fido promptly pushed them both into the wall and Robin couldn't help but feel a bit better. He had the woman he loved most in the world in his arms and the furry beast, who doubled as her additional protector, was also pleased to see him. There are some that would see this as a form of domestic bliss and, despite everything that had happened that day, he could see why. Olivia managed to get her arm free and pushed her glasses back up her nose in that way she did.

"I thought we could take Fido for his walk a little earlier than usual," she said as she fought to get the lead attached to his collar. Robin knew the real reason – she was increasingly worried about taking him out on her own as he'd already pulled her over twice. Luckily, Robin was much stronger. While he didn't particularly want to, he knew he should at least go for a walk with her on this occasion: it might be easier talking and walking rather than talking and staring at one another.

"Okay, I'll put on my trainers," he announced.

Extra pleased at not having to handle Fido alone, Olivia intertwined her fingers through Robin's as they let Fido pull them down the street towards his favourite local park. Well, it was the only one so … favourite by default, really. She shivered.

"I am not looking forward to winter," she confided, thinking about the fear she had of walking Fido on ice. "So, you must be wondering what I was texting you about earlier?"

"Today they told us our positions are in jeopardy," he blurted. He'd tried to concentrate on the best delivery of his bad tidings, but he'd utterly failed to come up with anything suitable. Then, unable to hold it in any longer, he'd just said it. He immediately felt her look up at him, but he kept his eyes on where they were walking.

"What?" she asked incredulously, as anyone would. He explained more thoroughly, giving her all the details. Olivia had been wondering why Robin had not enquired about her text – now she knew. She listened as he elaborated on what he planned to do about it. That was the thing about Robin, she knew – he was a thinker. She was more of a wonderer – she'd look at him and wonder what the hell he was thinking! He always had a plan. She was more than capable of coming up with her own plans, but it was good to know that your partner was also proficient at planning.

As they threw the stick for Fido and watched him tear up and down the playing field, all joy and obliviousness, they talked it through. Truth was, Robin had never particularly liked the job as it wasn't what he wanted to do. All right, he didn't really know what he wanted to do, not everyone does and there's nothing wrong with that. He'd been at the firm long enough to know that that wasn't it. As much fun as climbing corporate ladders was, there were just too many snakes sometimes. He had nothing against snakes, all life is sacred; that being said, they do add an undesired level of danger to the otherwise precarious world of ladder climbing.

Olivia offered to grammar check his *curriculum vitae* and volunteered to dispose of Fido's poop bag – how was that for foreplay? Normally, they only spent about forty-five minutes in the park, but they'd had such a lot to talk about that the twilight was encroaching by the time they headed for home. Clinging to Robin's arm as usual, Olivia told him that it would all be okay. His news had startled her, but she knew they had some time to make whatever moves they needed to.

It was only later, when they were in bed and Fido had been banished to his basket and blanket, that it occurred to Robin that he wasn't the only one who had something to talk about.

"Sorry," he said, deactivating his eBook. "Your text? You said something about something interesting?"

"Oh yes," she answered. She told him about the lone survivor of the morning's post.

"A codicil?" he frowned, not familiar with the word.

"Yes, I didn't know what it was either. My dad says it's an addition to a last will and testament. An amendment of sorts – like a last-minute change to a pre-existing will. It's super weird."

"A will? Who's dead?" he asked, bewildered.

"This is the crazy part – I really have no idea. Someone called Jack Tomlinson," she answered. They snuggled together after turning out the light.

"I don't know anyone called Jack Tomlinson," he said, knowing she already knew that.

"Me neither – sounds like we're never going to, either," she murmured. "Anyway, we need to contact a lady by the name of Polly-Ann Smyth for further details."

# CHAPTER TWO

# Forgettable for All the Right Reasons

Saturday mornings were always slow and cumbersome, like a train traversing a leaf-ridden track. Similar to a bug crawling up your leg. Akin to a committee trying to make a decision ... However, it was at least restful. Tea, toast and a boiled egg were a great way to start a day – even if it *was* nearly noon. A short trip through social media, aka home of the anonymuncules and their algorithmically challenged bots. A quick catch up on the news – often laced with a solid helping of propaganda – and the tone for the day was set.

First order of business after a cursory glance at the job listings was to talk to Olivia's father, Alexander, to decide what to do regarding the codicil. Despite their divorce, Olivia and Robin still got on well with both her parents. And, in the case of Alexander at least, it was always handy to be friends with a lawyer. Granted, he was focused mainly on corporate law, but he was well versed in all other disciplines, too. So, after Robin had dashed off a few job application emails, Olivia grabbed the phone. They sat opposite one another at the kitchen table, Fido slobbering ceaselessly beside them.

"As I said yesterday, I'm not a probate lawyer, so for more details you have to call the number provided and speak with this Polly-Ann Smyth. Haven't you done that yet?" Olivia rolled her eyes as Robin echoed the question faux judgementally.

"You know I didn't because I was waiting for you," she hissed playfully. She mischievously adjusted a coaster, deliberately upsetting the natural order of the universe, and giggled as Robin moved it back obsessively.

"Be careful, please, someone has died and there are legal ramifications. Please try not to agree to anything until you have the big picture," warned Alexander, prudently. "Arguably, it would be wise to have someone present with you when you call her but, as it's a last will and testament we're concerned with, I'm just as curious as you are. Robin, you're quite sure you know nothing of this person?"

"Absolutely," he confirmed, nodding. "It's all very odd."

"Call me back when you've spoken to her and we'll take it from there," he suggested.

"Thanks, Dad, bye," sighed Olivia. After the call was ended, there was a beat of silence as she dialled the number.

"You're still okay with us using your phone for this?" Robin asked again, considerately. She shrugged.

"I doubt it will make much difference," she sighed. They looked at one another as her finger hovered over the call button – they were just putting it off and they both knew it. They'd already googled the number and it seemed to be a personal mobile phone number with no scamming reported.

She called it but they reached an answerphone. Robin let out a breath he'd been holding in. He wasn't exactly sure why they were so tense about this, but they were and no one answering at all had been the very definition of an anti-climax.

"Try again later, I suppose," he said as she leaned back on the sofa.

"Maybe I should have called yesterday," she muttered, concerned.

"Do you think she's expecting us? She might be just as confused as we are," he said, knowing Olivia couldn't know the answer to that.

They jumped as her phone started to ring and vibrate loudly. Fido barked wildly.

"Answer it!"

"No, you answer it, it's your phone!"

"Coward!" she snapped, psyching herself up a second time. As if on cue, all the other devices in the apartment began to ring too, raising the anxiety levels substantially. Robin grabbed it and answered.

"Hello?"

"Hello," said a man's voice. Robin put it on loudspeaker. "Did you just call this number?"

"Hi, yes we did," responded Robin, instinctively glancing at the codicil. "We're trying to get hold of someone called Polly-Ann Smyth."

"Ah, this is Peter Barnes here, let me get her for you. You wouldn't happen to be Robin Meadows and Olivia Higgins, would you?"

"That's right," was Olivia's rejoinder, unsure if this was a good sign or not.

"Hello," said a croaky voice. "Is that Robin and Olivia?" They said it was. "Wonderful, please feel free to call me Kat. You'll be wanting to know what all this is about, I presume?"

"Yes," said Olivia, pleased they were getting somewhere. "We got this codicil and …"

"Ah, it is as it says … as beneficiaries, you're required to come to Tomlinson Hall and be present when the last will and testament of Jack Tomlinson is read–"

"I see," interrupted Olivia. "Yes, we understand that part, and we will do that, but …" she hesitated. "We're a bit confused, Kat. We aren't related to the deceased – as far as we can tell, we were not even known to him."

"I too have reached that conclusion," agreed Kat. "Perhaps more will be revealed during the reading."

"So, you really have no idea who we are or why we've been included?" Olivia asked, a bit frustrated.

"It's a mystery to us, too. The vicar and I have discussed it extensively and we can't fathom the link, but there must be one," she answered, her voice getting stronger now.

"Who was Jack Tomlinson exactly?" That question came from Robin. He was frowning as he listened intently to the exchange.

"He was the owner of Tomlinson Hall and he resided here until 1985. Since then, while there has been much speculation over the years about his movements, he has just been declared legally dead," she replied, slowly.

"So, as that's based on him having disappeared so long ago, we don't know he's dead for sure?" asked Robin, frowning.

"No! No one has heard from him in over twelve years," she said, sadly. "If he were still to be alive, I think it's safe to say he's not intending to come back."

"And we don't know what drove him away, do we?" he asked, in an undertone. Kat didn't answer.

"Okay, we'll come up tomorrow first thing, and talk about this face to face. The address is on the codicil," said Olivia. Robin raised his eyebrows.

"That would be wonderful," Kat said, much relief in her voice.

When the call was over, Robin reminded her that he had work on the Tuesday so he could only stay there one night. It was a Bank Holiday, after all.

"It won't take long," she argued.

"But the will reading isn't until next week! We'd have to stay ages! Why do we have to go now ...?" he complained.

"Aren't you curious?" she demanded. "Don't you want to know

what all this is about?"

"Well, yes, but not so much that I will wreck my schedule to do it!" he protested. She crossed her arms and pulled a face.

"And what about *my* schedule?" she enquired, looking hurt.

"Don't!" he scoffed, wagging his finger at her. "You work from home, you can work from there, it's not the same."

"Take some holiday! You're owed some. This is important!"

"Are you mad? I'm about to lose my job, I need to keep my finger on the pulse just in case something important develops," he argued. She sighed, lowering her head a little.

"That's fair," she admitted, not wanting to tell him the real reason she wanted him to stay on with her. She didn't want to stay somewhere alone for that long – particularly in a place she wasn't familiar with. He saw the truth and pulled her in for a hug.

"I'll be back on Friday after work, I promise," he insisted, softly. "You'll be fine, and you'll have Fido …"

He trailed off as he watched the dog gently gnawing on her slipper. Maybe having Fido wasn't such a good thing after all, but they couldn't leave him behind.

"My mum always said I'd want to move to the country when I got older," she murmured sadly.

"So …"

"No, I don't want to move, it took us ages to find this flat, I just know what she'll think," she said. Robin had no idea why what Olivia's mother thought mattered at all, but he didn't question it. Their relationship could be tricky to understand. They loved each other, just as a mother and daughter should, but they did argue occasionally.

# CHAPTER THREE

## The Twin Fates of Primrose

The M25 circled London in all directions and had a mesmeric, recurring quality. One motorway looks much like another, all things considered. You might be at junction thirteen but, unless you knew it well, you might easily mistake it for junction fourteen. It had been Robin's idea to circle around London on the M25, take junction twenty-three, and seek out the elusive Albany-on-Lea. Apparently Google Maps had missed it out completely and the GPS had just made a gargling noise when they'd entered the postcode. It was clear that once they had escaped the magical motorway, things would get a little difficult, but he remained confident. Olivia had the map, after all, and even though the village didn't seem to be on it, everything nearby was, so it should be easy enough.

As always when behind the wheel of a car, Robin was transported back to that rainy day. It was while driving that Primrose had met his fate, after all. January 12$^{th}$ 1997, had been an ordinary Thursday for a lot of people. Well, if we're being honest, despite what happened, it was still ordinary; after all, death is ordinary. Imagine the chaos if no one ever died! You'd never get a parking space again, that was for sure. In any case, it had been raining quite heavily and, at first, that was what everyone had thought might have caused the accident. Roads slick with water and left-over ice was never a great thing. 'Wasn't the start of a goodyear' was a joke Robin quickly got tired of.

It must have rained for the entire year as far as Robin's memory was concerned. A large drip of rain had, by hook or by crook, got past his shirt collar and had run down his spine, making him shiver. It had thrown itself from the tip of one of the huge black umbrellas above him and he'd broken its fall to the mud. Primrose had died in a car crash; he was the only one in the car at the time and no other vehicles appeared to be involved. He'd not been drinking or anything – the first theory was that he'd either lost control and crashed, swerved to avoid an animal, or fallen asleep at the wheel. Only later was it determined that he'd had a heart attack.

This then led to the melancholic query: did the attack cause the crash or the other way around? It was one of those Schrodinger type situations, at least it was in Robin's young mind, hence the twin fates of Primrose. In the real world, both had happened but, for reasons unknown, an exact chain of events escaped everyone. An unofficial veteran of the Falklands conflict, Primrose had always been tough and severe, so the idea that he could be gone, just like that, was most disturbing. Not to mention that death in itself, through the eyes of a child, is just so offsetting. *What do you mean, no one knows what happens? I thought y'all knew everything!*

A puddle was forming on the coffin as the robed vicar began to speak. Robin could see his distorted reflection in it as he stared down. Each raindrop sent ripples out and away to prevent clarity – another lesson about perception from the cosmos. Can we see what it's trying to tell us? If the purpose of life was to have a purposeful life, then it would make sense that our reflections don't look the same as us. This is not what the priest said, but it might just as well have been for all the sense it made to Robin. All he knew for sure was that he'd never see Primrose again and that made him want to cry.

What had Primrose left behind? No wife and no children to speak of. No property, no legacy, not even some wise words. It seemed he'd lived and died and left no trace at all, squandered in oblivion, consigned to be forgotten and lost to time. Maybe that was why Robin had never allowed himself to forget him! Death was scary enough, but the idea of no one ever knowing you'd existed seemed worse somehow. Maybe that was why everyone wanted to make their mark – just to say that they had been there. Would there be anybody left to see them? If there was, would they understand? Would they do the same and repeat the cycle?

Robin was coaxed from his morbid reverie by the notes to a song and, more interestingly, Olivia's hand on his thigh. He glanced across but she wasn't looking at him, she was staring ahead at the dark clouds on the horizon. There was nothing metaphorical about those absolute units hovering there, looking ready to drop an entire ocean on them! Was it his imagination, or did he see a distant flicker of lightning? The song playing on the radio sounded ominous in the quiet of the car. *The End of the World* by Arthur Dent and Skeeter Davis. As Skeeter's soulful voice crackled through the speakers, Olivia seemed to get increasing tense and, as if in sympathy, so did he.

Robin gently put his hand on top of hers and she actually jumped, giggled emotionally and looked like she was going to cry or something.

"Babe, what's wrong?" he asked, letting out a horrified little chortle. "Did we forget something?"

"I don't know," she said, shaking her head and pushing her glasses up her nose. "I just felt … weird. I had a strange feeling … That song didn't help either."

Maybe this was her subtle way of telling him she didn't want the radio on anymore.

"Do you want me to turn …?" he began, not sure what else he could do.

"No, it's fine," she smiled, not very convincingly. The awkward silence between them returned. No… not awkward, anything but that!

"Your app didn't mention that?" he murmured, changing the subject to the weather. Classic Englishman – don't you worry about anything, have you noticed the precipitation in the air? Olivia muttered, as if she'd somehow missed it.

"It did not," she said, scrolling on her phone. "It's not mentioning it now, either: according to this, it's meant to be blue skies."

Robin shook his head slowly. "So much for technology."

Olivia turned in her chair and gave Fido a reassuring stroke. Despite the chaos that he often seemed to cause in a vehicle, he was curled up and fast asleep. It was unusual, but quite a relief.

"Five more miles until the junction," Robin smiled, trying to cheer her up. "Then we get to the exciting part." She managed a smile.

"It will be nice to see what all this is about," she replied. On reflection, he realised that her remark was not as positive as it sounded. She opened Google Maps and began to find their position.

"Okay, we need to head for High Barnet, so … third exit on the second roundabout," she directed. He held in the sigh and pulled an exaggerated smile.

"Thank you," he growled jokingly. She glared friskily at him.

"I have two words for you: Great Yarmouth!" she stated, knowing how much he loved it when she dug up the past.

"I stopped and asked for directions, just like you wanted," he grumbled, cringing slightly. They could laugh about this now, but at the time they had been almost strangling each other. Ah, young love!

"Indeed you did … fifty-six minutes later," she reminded him pointedly.

"One more like that and you're walking the rest of the way."

"Might get there faster," she giggled.

He hooted in a wounded tone, shaking his head.

"That's it, nothing like a bit of road rage to finish the journey," he replied. "And you'd behaved so well …" Pulling off, they laughed their way up the exit ramp.

He followed her instructions, heading off towards High Barnet.

"Stagg Hill," she murmured, peering around like a meerkat, trying to read all the signs at once. They passed a bus stop on the opposite side of the road, then a driveway on their left. That was when, now that they were directly under the clouds, the heavens opened. Olivia did not like storms at the best of times and, while Robin was largely indifferent to them, even he was taken aback by the force of the deluge. Fido stirred and looked around briefly, too. It was getting so dark they could barely make out the cable masts in the fields.

Robin slowed down a little and turned on the headlights. The sky lit up suddenly as lightning arced its way through the clouds. Olivia stared out mutely in anxiety. As the rain hammered the car, Robin concentrated on the road, watching the drops bounce off the concrete.

"Maybe we should go back," she suggested, not serious.

"*It's a trap!*" he jested, sensing she needed a little comfort. "Roundabout coming up, where next?" She scrolled on her phone again.

"Waggon Road to Dancers Hill and it should be somewhere … somewhere there," she trailed off, knowing this was the vague part. "So go right, please."

"Ooh, got a please that time," he smiled, trying to calm her down. The thunder sounded and she swore as she glanced up. The rain became heavier still.

"Should we stop somewhere and wait this out?" she asked, nervously. "I can barely see the road."

"Well, there's no way of knowing how long it's going to rain for, and we're really close now, probably ten minutes away or so." Committing to a number with Olivia was a major faux pas, he knew – she got funny when the actual numbers were different to the ones he gave her. They were out of the built-up part and in the countryside again, and that creepy feeling that they'd had earlier seemed to return.

The rain became patchy and then just big drops. They passed some more buildings, but this wasn't the village yet. It was somewhere around this point that – neither of them would ever be able to pinpoint precisely where – that they somehow got lost. Ten minutes, Robin had said, and believed, at least at the time when he'd said it. Over an hour later and they were heading down yet another country lane, utterly clueless about where they were or where they were going. The map app crashed – absolutely useless, there was no signal, technology had failed again – and the rain was getting worse once again.

Olivia had resorted to an old paper map from the back – a hardback AA special from 2009. Luckily, unlike many of her generation, she did know how to read a map that wasn't on a screen. Nevertheless, the village didn't appear to be listed.

"This is stupid!" she declared, having reached the end of her tether. She pointed aggressively at a grid reference. "It should be right there!"

"We can't be far away!" insisted Robin, equally baffled.

"We should have gone left at the last junction!" she hissed.

"You said go right!" he yelled, annoyed.

"Yes, I know, don't yell at me, I didn't mean to get us lost!" she shouted back. "I was only following what I thought the map was telling me."

"You tried turning it the right way up?" he couldn't resist firing back. She glared at him and then her lip trembled, and he immediately knew he'd taken it too far.

"Look, it's not your fault and nothing has happened, people get lost every day," he backtracked, apologetically.

"I swear … it should have been this way," she said, her eyes wet.

"Maybe it is," he sighed, trying not to sound too exasperated. He saw a driveway ahead and pulled in. He turned to her, and they hugged.

"I'm sorry, I didn't mean to shout at you, I was getting impatient," he said, rubbing her back tenderly.

"I just don't understand how we went wrong," she said, wiping her eyes. She didn't like being lost.

"Don't worry," he said, smiling encouragingly. "We'll find it eventually." He held her hands and squeezed them gently. "It's the damage you've just done to the feminist cause that worries me. I mean, screwing up something simple like navigation, oh my God!"

She laughed. "I'll have to delete my Twitter account," she giggled, shaking her head. "Seriously though … I genuinely, *really*, have no idea how we went wrong." They looked at the map together and, assuming it was accurate, Robin admitted that he'd have done the same.

"I mean, whoever made this map should clearly be shot," she jested more cheerfully. She'd been worried that he'd spot something she'd overlooked and make her feel very silly. He wouldn't mean to make her feel that way, she knew he wouldn't, but she would feel angry with herself. Robin tapped the steering wheel as he cogitated and stared out at the rain. Fido whined.

"Glad I made these now," she said, passing him a cheese sandwich. "Pickle?"

"Are you asking me or addressing me?" he chuckled. "Not now, thanks, might want to save something for dinner if we're still lost by then." She gave him a wide-eyed look. "We won't be," he hastily added.

Robin propped the map up on the dashboard before trying and failing to get a signal.

"If we went back to that turnstile we passed and go down the turn-off, we should end up back on the A road, right?" he asked.

"Don't ask me, I'm just the navigator," she mumbled through her sandwich. She handed him a crisp packet, which he took. She then began to pass some beef jerky over to Fido, her hand getting thoroughly licked in the process. There was only the hammering of the rain now that the engine was off, and it was oddly restful. Robin squirmed a little in his seat, wanting to get out and stretch his legs.

There was, of course, the chance they would be unable to find Albany-on-Lea, no matter how long they roamed the country roads. There was some spare fuel in the back, but he didn't think Olivia would be up for spending the night driving round in circles. Again, he stared balefully at the map. They should have found it, really. He was just starting to wonder if perhaps the whole thing had been filched from the rejected line of the Department of Ornate Pranks, and that Albany-on-Lea didn't exist at all, when a pair of headlights caught his attention.

Looming out of the darkness and rumbling loudly, a tractor arrived and halted a few metres in front of them. Robin and Olivia watched in surprise as a man opened the door, waved at them, and then began to descend. They exchanged a look as Robin cracked the window open a little. Engine trouble perhaps? An escaped sheep?

"You all right?" asked the man, as he got closer. "A flat?" He had a strong accent that Robin couldn't place or imitate. The thick, grey beard also played some role in obscuring its oral delicacies. Before Robin could answer, Olivia leapt onto his appearance like a lifeline.

"Hi, we're actually lost, we can't …" she began.

"Ahh, you wouldn't by any chance be trying to get to Albany-on-Lea, would you now?" he asked, squinting a little.

"Yes, we are, how did you …?" started Robin.

"Lot of people have trouble finding that old place," he elaborated, with an unconcerned wave of his hand. "I'll lead the way; you follow me, and I'll take you straight to it. My farm is on the other side and while it has two by-passes, there's so little traffic that it won't take me much longer."

"Thanks so much, you're a diamond!" smiled Olivia, really pleased that this nightmare would soon be over.

Robin said nothing after waving the man away, and followed the tractor, not sure what to think. Stroke of luck, certainly, but was it bad or good? Olivia strained to see through the rain as the farmer led them through what felt like a rabbit warren of roads, tracks and, at one stage, a lane that seemed to snake its way through a forest. Then, just when they were on the verge of concluding they'd followed a serial killer, and it was time to run for their lives, a sign appeared. *Welcome to Albany-on-Lea*, it said, and cottages appeared on either side of them.

"Yes!" hissed Olivia, pumping her fist in triumph. Trying his best to see through the rain, Robin studied the area. There was a church and a village green and what looked like a war memorial in the centre of the green. If you included the road they'd arrived on, there were only two other roads, each leading away from the green. The church stood to their left and it was possible to make out the graves beyond.

Across from the church was what looked like a pub. The warm glow of quiet, dry hospitality seemed to beckon to them. The tractor stopped and the farmer once again came out to speak to them.

"Welcome to Albany-on-Lea," he announced, with a thumbs up. "You'll be alright now."

"Thank you so much," gushed Olivia, genuinely. "I don't think we'd ever have found this place without your help."

"You ever need a favour, you know where to come," assured Robin, putting down the window and shaking the man's hand, who said his name was Mick.

"No, I do not," he laughed. "Visiting family, are you?"

"Not exactly," replied Robin, not sure how much he should say. This man could be anyone.

"We're supposed to go to somewhere called Tomlinson Hall," Olivia explained. "Do you know where that is?" The man's expression seemed to change ever so slightly, but then returned to his previous countenance almost instantly. Olivia couldn't see it from where she was sitting but Robin caught the look and hoped that it was nothing.

"I do; it's about a mile up that road on the right," he said, pointing to the other side of the village green.

"Brilliant, thanks again …" she continued.

"That pub any good?" asked Robin, nodding towards it. The farmer paused as if weighing up his answer.

"The Old New Inn, it's called," he explained, ignoring the rain completely now. For a second, he just looked exhausted. "I know the owner very well and she's usually very welcoming to guests."

"Right …" said Robin, sensing something sinister. *Usually*? And what about the clientele?

"Probably best you go straight to the Hall if they're expecting you there," suggested the farmer in a tone that occupied territory 'twixt the polite and the firm. "I'll leave you now, and good luck." With that, he turned and went back to his tractor, a huge hulk of a man trudging forwards steadily. He headed off into the storm, the huge wheels unbothered by the puddles.

Olivia looked at Robin, who just sat there, holding the steering wheel.

"What?" she asked, knowing something was up.

"I think he was trying to warn us against going in there," he explained, nodding towards the pub. Olivia thought about it.

"No, he just looked a bit off when we mentioned we were going to the Hall," she reasoned. She could be right, Robin knew, but he still felt that his conclusion about the pub was more accurate.

"We can always come back if you want to have dinner here," she suggested.

"Maybe we will," Robin said noncommittally, starting to drive again.

Unlike finding the village, locating the Hall itself was a piece of cake. Its wide driveway led through a garden which, if it were summer, would have looked spectacular. The Hall itself was a large, intimidating looking structure. At the end of the driveway, it stood as if indifferent to the ravages of the storm. After the engine fell silent, they stared up at the huge building, a little spellbound. Lights were on inside, so it was obvious someone was home; yet, contrasting sharply with the rest of the village, this light did not seem so inviting. Less of a *do come in* and more of a *what do you want?* Then, as if on cue, the rain stopped. It didn't lessen over minutes nor peter out over a few seconds ... it just ended.

Fido let out a low growl and Olivia shivered. "Well," she sighed, more breezily than she felt. "We're here."

"Where is here?" Robin mumbled, still staring up at the place. She rolled her eyes, much more confident now that she knew where she was. She pushed her glasses up her nose, opened the door and stepped out decisively. Splash! Robin followed her example but managed to avoid the puddle. While she attached the lead to Fido's collar, Robin approached the grand doorway. He took in the text over the archway casually. *Home sweet home, where the hearts are, where it is good to be.* He saw a chain that had to be connected to a bell within, and thought about pulling on it.

Olivia, dragged by Fido, caught up.

"That sounds wholesome," she said, also reading the inscription.

"I wonder how old this place is."

"Older than us," he mumbled, attempting levity. Slowly, she extended her free hand and reached for the chain. She paused as she realised he was watching her.

"What?" she asked, withdrawing her hand.

"I don't know," he said, shrugging.

"Do you not want me to?"

"I don't know."

"Robin!" she tittered, not knowing how to answer him. "We know someone's inside, and this is the traditional way of asking for admittance, isn't it?"

"I've just got a funny feeling," he confessed, not knowing which words to use. She raised her eyebrows, knowing he wasn't referring to travel sickness. "Like, we're not meant to be here, as if we're somehow … intruding." She didn't want to tell him she felt very similar.

"Well, we kind of are," she pointed out. "We were invited, we have a right, of sorts, to be here and we've come a long way so …"

"Yeah, I know, I don't know what's wrong with me."

"We've had a stressful day," was her rational response. "We're in a … like … we're in a foreign place and the weather is being weird. I'm sure we're just reacting to that."

She did sound very convincing, but he knew it was an act. She was as uncomfortable as he was, she was just doing a much better job of hiding it. Either way, only one option would mean progress. He grabbed the chain and pulled. A distant, but still somehow loud, bell rang. They exchanged a glance or two at the sound of approaching footsteps. They heard locks being pulled back and keys jangling as someone began to unlock the door. With a creak worthy of any big budget horror movie, the old door inched open.

# CHAPTER FOUR

# Tomlinson Hall

# Part One: We Are All Made of Dust

Notes from *Chronicles of Barnet – Legacy of the Tomlinsons* by Professor of History, Tracey Stannett MSc (1961-2014)

*History rhymes with mystery and the first mystery about Tomlinson Hall, a large estate located near the village of Albany-on-Lea, is that it's unknown who built it. No one can even agree on a date, but it certainly wasn't listed in the Domesday Book Great Survey of 1086. No note of it was made in the accounts of those who fought in the Battle of Barnet in 1471, either, despite the conflict taking place in and around the nearby market town of Chipping Barnet. The Hall embodies the dark age tradition of springing from nowhere.*

*The first reference of the Hall came from a source in 1487 on a receipt for an aged delivery which tells us next to nothing about the Hall itself. Was it under construction then? Had they just finished building it and were celebrating their success with a flagon or two? Or had the Hall already been standing for centuries? As an avid historian, I have a loathing for the phrase 'no one knows' yet I am forced to use it here.*

*Architecture, you'd think, would be the key, should documentation fail us, to learn more! It's often an accurate way of dating structures, particularly if the architect is known. Frequently, people expound about the brick and the sash windows of the Georgian era, the gothic grandeur of the Victorian age, or even the* brutalism of the nineteen sixties. That's without delving into the deeds of the architects themselves. Glasshouse symbolism of the twenty-twenties, anyone? Let he who is without sin cast the first stone … Again, here, Tomlinson Hall offers little in the way of clues. This may be due to the actions of an industrialist known as Edward Tomlinson, somewhere around 1799.

Legend has it, for there is no proof, that after he acquired the property, he spent his first evening there burning all records on the instructions of the previous owner. While this does explain why there are seemingly no historical references to the property, there is no proof that this happened. Nor is there sufficient evidence that, even if this did occur, that the previous owner, whoever they were, didn't do it themselves. This would make more sense as, unless they knew Edward Tomlinson very well, it's unlikely they'd trust him to do something like that on their behalf.

The door opened to reveal Peter Barns. If ever there was a physical, corporeal personification of average, he was it. Typical height, middle-aged, greying brown hair, and clothes entirely bereft of symbols or logos. He was wearing a brown fleece, blue jeans and an understated pair of slippers. His face bore evidence of laughter in the form of wrinkles and dimples and his brown eyes examined Robin and Olivia.

"Afternoon, how can I help?" he asked. They easily recognised his voice from the phone call of the previous day.

"Olivia and Robin, we spoke yesterday," explained Robin, extending his hand, though, in all honesty, it was hard to believe they would be mistaken for anyone else. Peter shook his hand firmly before shaking Olivia's.

"Of course. And is your friend over there friendly?" he asked as Fido tried to lick his face off. Olivia had been worried that Fido might not be allowed inside, or that there could be other pets. People had allergies to think about, too, and she'd forgotten to ask.

"Fido!" commanded Robin, pointing to the floor. Fido sat down more promptly than ever before, making Olivia smile with pride.

Finally, Fido was starting to listen. That online training course hadn't been complete baloney then! They had insisted that dogs had star signs and encouraged owners not to feed their dog meat. In addition to that, they had recommended all the most expensive toys … Olivia had checked. Investing in a plaything for that dog was a little like choosing to become a paying member of a political party: reckless and, some would say, wasteful. She would never encourage such wanton luxury nor rash frivolities, plus she didn't like the idea.

At six foot two, Robin was taller than Peter by a few inches, but the doorway proved ample size for the four of them. Beyond Peter was a tidy looking entrance hall with a stairway rising up towards an upper floor where it linked to a wooden banister. All along the stairs were portraits of men and women, along with other paintings. Even a tapestry or two hung down as if waiting to be inspected and admired. Peter explained that he was the caretaker, and it was obvious that he was good at looking after the place. He divested them of their cagoules and the rest of their wind-cheating apparatus with a professional flare, the sort of thing you would associate with a butler rather than a caretaker.

"Please, the north living room is this way. You are no doubt tired from your journey. Would you like some refreshment?" he asked, leading the way to the left. Exchanging a bewildered glance, Robin and Olivia followed him into the large room beyond. This was a far cry from their London apartment. High, decorated ceilings, huge armchairs that were obviously rivals of the one in *Game of Thrones*. There was what looked like a musket, although Robin wasn't sure, it could be a rifle, on the wall above a grand fireplace. Olivia was rather spellbound.

"Take a seat, Kat is running late," he explained. He gave a sort of chortle then his face became sad. "Not as quick as she used to be."

"Did you say the north living room?" asked Olivia, trying to stop Fido from joining her on the chair.

"I did," he said, nudging an old basket out from behind the chair. It contained a blanket and an old pillow. "Not used this in a while. Here." He beckoned to Fido who, much to Robin's surprise, obeyed, got into the basket and lay down. Peter picked up on their mutual awe.

"I've always loved dogs and it seems they've always loved me," he said, stroking the big fellow.

"So …?" Olivia asked, trying to remember what she was talking about.

"There is a south living room, yes, just across the entrance hallway there. I'll show you around after if you like. Tea?" he offered, heading out.

"Please," managed Olivia, still rather stunned. It didn't look this big from outside, somehow.

"It's like Mary Poppins's house," smirked Robin, sitting opposite her.

"Or a TARDIS," she concurred. They stared at one another, trying to judge their situation by observing their own reactions. A common technique, but not all that useful during joint hallucinations, obviously.

"I don't know if I like this," she confided in an undertone, clearly torn. Nothing had gone wrong since arriving, but there was an undeniable curdle of an undercurrent that insisted on spoiling the hot cross bun. A disquiet, an unease. They looked around the large room and could only compare it to a stately home or estate which, they supposed, this was.

"It's … I don't really know," he said, slouching in defeat. "This is a hell of a chair, though … wouldn't want to stub your toe on this beast." She giggled a little.

"You wouldn't have a toe left," she reflected, studying its monstrous legs. They gazed around in an awestruck silence at the room they'd found themselves in. Of course, whether they'd lost themselves before finding themselves was up for debate, but you can't make an omelette without cracking an egg.

A dresser of silverware, a cabinet of drinks accompanied by their many lavish decanters, several foot stools and coffee tables: it was a cornucopia of old-fashioned style and opulence and that meant a lot. A mini chandelier dominated the centre of the ceiling, and almost concealed the delicate patterns above it. It seemed to glimmer perpetually, undimmed by the passing of time or water.

"Do you think this whole place is like this?" she half whispered. She was starting to think she knew the reason for this discomfort – a feeling of not belonging. No, more than that, it was as if they were trespassing or something. They clearly weren't as they'd been invited in! Nevertheless, the feeling remained, mysterious and stubborn. Robin glanced at Fido, who lay in his new bed peacefully – evidently nothing was worrying him. That made Robin relax a bit and he nodded to the dog to make Olivia look. She did, and pulled that face she did when falling in love with a cute fur ball. Not so much a ball as a globe by this stage, it should be noted.

Peter appeared again a few minutes later, pushing a trolley ahead of him, clinking as he went.

"How was your journey?" he asked, conscious of the uncomfortable silence. "Weather's anxiously inclement, isn't it?" A banal chitchat ensued – a perfect example of strangers' stilted, post-salutation, conversation. Kat still hadn't arrived, and they were two cups of tea down! At last, when yet another pregnant pause patently refused to give birth to seamless social skills, Peter gave up and insisted he give them a tour of the property. There is some truth that the gap 'twixt generations is more like a chasm where the token gestures from either side plummet into. They might well have been speaking different languages. Yet Tomlinson Hall was about to bring its true influence to bear on the situation.

Peter led the new trio back into the entrance hall. He showed them the south living room first which was similar to the north in shape, only with different styled furniture and a different arrangement, so actually it was nothing like its counterpart. They strolled through the kitchen, wine cellar, pantry, sitting room, study, lower guest bedroom, en suite bathroom, and visitor's bathroom, only to end up back in the entrance hall again. Everything downstairs was decorated, fully furnished and extravagant in the extreme. There were two other staircases, both spiral in design, and both occupying the opposite ends of the north and south wings.

Peter began to lead them up the stairs and Robin took in the portraits of men and women on the wall. Their eyes … it's a cliché really … but he could have sworn they moved.

"And this," smiled Peter, stopping at the first one. "This is the original master of the house, to the best of our knowledge. Edward Tomlinson." Robin and Olivia gazed at the painting in genuine awe. A powerful looking aristocratic man stared back at them forbiddingly. For a man dead nearly two hundred years, that was a hell of a glare.

"He looks imposing," said Olivia, carefully.

"Industrialist, you know, many say with royal connections. He held some balls in here, that's for sure …" explained Peter. Robin and Olivia exchanged a look at that and managed not to laugh.

"Both King George the third and the fourth stayed here," he said, not looking away from the portrait. "Back in 1816." He paused and then gave a little laugh. "Probably still celebrating Waterloo."

"1815?" guessed Robin, trying to remember. Peter faced him, impressed.

"Yes, correct, that was the year, not that either of them actually fought in it, of course," he said, moving up a few steps to a portrait of a woman. "And his wife, Mary." Olivia stared up at the woman, admiring the hair and the dress, but unable to quite ignore the eyes.

"They're like real eyes," she said, with an uneasy laugh. Peter said nothing to that but moved on to the next painting. This was another man, similar to the first.

"Henry, the first son of Edward and Mary," he said. The man had the same mane of brown curly hair, same eyes as his father, but he had a little smile that seemed to make him more human than his dad.

"His wife?" guessed Olivia, pointing to the next painting of a fair-haired lady in white.

"Indeed. Gwendoline was her name," he smiled, a tinge of sadness on his face now. "Died the same year as her husband – broken heart, so it is held." Olivia gasped and even Robin felt a twinge of sympathy.

"When?" Olivia almost whispered, staring into the blue eyes before her.

"1891," he sighed, also looking at the portrait.

"And this is presumably the next generation?" asked Robin, motioning them to beyond the halfway point on the stairs. Another man, but this one had shorter hair and a more severe countenance than his predecessor.

"Another happy couple," smiled Peter, moving to stand before the next woman's portrait. "Thomas and Mary."

"Who's that?" asked Olivia, indicating another picture beyond. This portrait broke the established order so far, being another woman next to Mary.

"Ah, another Mary, I'm afraid. This was Thomas's older sister. No one really knows what happened to her, but it's believed she went to live in the States."

"Right …" said Olivia, not sure what else to say.

"You can tell they're related, look at those eyes," observed Robin, still a little hyper-focused on them. He'd detected that the only painting's eyes which had not looked like a real person were those of the sister, the one who allegedly went to America. Maybe the painter had been working from another painting rather than the actual person?

"The Tomlinsons were said to have very piercing stares," continued Peter, seeming to enjoy their interest. "Like as if they could see straight through you – cut right through your spirit like a blade. Drill down to the centre of your soul and confront the real you directly …"

Robin and Olivia shared a perplexed glance.

"Know them personally, did you?" asked Robin, innocently.

"Only the last of them; the rest I know through story alone," he answered, somewhat cryptically. They moved on to the next two depictions towards the end of the stairs and the hallway above.

"Arthur and Suzanna," he said, staring at them.

"Thank goodness, I don't think I could handle another Mary," smiled Olivia, trying to inject some levity into this rather serious discussion. No one reacted to that, and she was forced to stare into the couple's eyes. The clothing worn was becoming more modern now but for some reason, this wasn't making things any more relatable.

Arthur looked much more like the great grandfather, Edward, only this time with a short pointy beard. His moustache was of the typically Edwardian variety, which made sense, given that he died in 1932. Suzanna was the most regal looking of the women so far, with the possible exception of Gwendoline who sported a number of jewels, pearly necklaces and rings. Her gaze seemed as imperious as Arthur's was stern. These were the last two that were actual paintings; from then on, it was blown-up photographs.

"Henry and Anne," said Peter, nodding toward the first large picture. This was a further departure from the norm so far in that they were photographed together, with their arms around each other, grinning at the camera. Olivia smiled a little in relief – these two looked much more friendly. There was another couple next to them, taken in a similar style.

"Georgina Ward and her husband Peter Ward. Georgina was a Tomlinson before marriage," he elaborated. "The four of them were a rolling party, apparently ..."

"They look it," agreed Robin, grinning.

"Until Georgina's death in 1941," he continued. Robin's smile vanished.

"Oh," he managed, awkwardly.

"No, no, they helped Peter, Henry and Anne did, always inviting him around and supporting him through his loss. The death did not break the friendship and Georgina wouldn't have wanted it to. There was a war on, and she died doing her job," he elucidated, letting Robin know he'd not hurt any feelings. There was a fondness in his tone and Robin wondered for a second who the fondness was directed at, the dead woman or himself. "Indeed, Peter was a comfort somewhat to Anne when Henry died, although ..." He paused, halting as if peering over a precipice. He moved from the top of the stairs to a photograph of two boys.

"Edward and Jack Tomlinson," he said, his voice now sadder than ever. He pointed to the boy on the right. "That's Jack, the one who's just been declared legally dead." Robin and Olivia moved closer to look. A fair-haired lad with a boyish grin, looking very much like he could be any boy in the world. What else had they been expecting? A baby dragon? Peter moved away, staring back down the stairs before slowly looking upwards towards the decorative ceiling, and gave a hopeful smile. In a voice too quiet for Robin and Olivia to hear, he implored, "They're here, just like you wanted. Please don't do anything stupid. I don't have the strength to do this again."

Lastly, he showed them the bedrooms and bathrooms that made

up the two wings upstairs. Unlike downstairs, the walls had fewer picture and hangings, the decorations were more mundane and the atmosphere somewhat colder. That was with one exception: the library. Packed with hundreds of books, antique wooden shelving and a walkway stretching right around it, it was spectacular. Here, in a glass display case, were Henry's World War One medals and his service revolver. The 1914-15 Star Medal, the British War Medal, and the Victory Medal. Finally, behind all of this was a sword with a golden hilt, and Robin immediately recognised it as the one Arthur Tomlinson was sporting in his painting.

"The Tomlinson blade," sighed Peter, admiring it with them. "Been in their family since around the 1850s. Henry carried it with him to war in France."

"Wow," said Olivia, transfixed. "The real thing."

"I don't know if he actually used it," added Peter with a slight grin.

"This is surreal," stated Robin, turning to take in all the books and shelves. "I mean … it's like a museum or something."

"It's a home, Robin, a very old home," he replied. "A lot of the other things were sold. This is the majority of what remains."

"Other things?" breathed Olivia, in wonder. How much more was there?

"Yes, the jewellery, the clothes, the art pieces, land and properties," he listed, easily. "Since 1985, things have not been so good for the Tomlinsons," he told them. "Though the decline began some years before that."

"That's … that's when Jack disappeared, right?" asked Olivia, remembering.

"Indeed."

"Hang on, what happened to Edward?" asked Robin, confused.

"Died the year before his brother vanished," said Peter, bowing his head a little.

"So …" began Olivia, realising they were still no closer to figuring out why they were there. Theories about murder and fleeing the country came unbidden into her thoughts.

A bell rang, making Olivia jump, and even Robin whirled a little. It seemed so much louder and echoey than it did from outside.

"Ah, that will be Kat," sighed Peter, as if relieved. "Though why she doesn't just use her key still baffles me. Please wait here." They waited until his footsteps had died away before saying anything.

"This place is sick," declared Olivia, still in awe. She glanced back at Robin who, unusually, was allowing his curiosity to get the better of him and was trying to get the display cabinet open.

"What are you doing?" she hissed, slapping his hands away.

"I was just looking. Anyway, it's locked," he complained, fending her off.

"Well, of course it is, you don't think he'd just leave us in here with that, do you?" she demanded, annoyed.

"Suppose not," he shrugged. "Don't really know what to think about any of this yet."

"Me neither," was her low response. "We still need to figure out why we've been invited."

Robin didn't answer and seemed to be in a reverie. She stared up at him.

"Babe?" she asked, trying to get his attention. "Why are you acting weird?" He snapped out of it.

"Sorry, I was …" he trailed off, again staring into the cabinet. Why did he feel so drawn to that sword? Why did he want to pick it up? Olivia was right, he *was* acting weird, something about this place was making everything peculiar. She frowned up at him and rubbed his face with her hand tenderly.

"What?" she blurted, worried.

"It's nothing," he said as voices came from outside.

Peter appeared in the doorway, followed by a small, white-haired old lady. Dressed completely in black, wielding a surprisingly sophisticated looking stick, she entered and smiled at the couple before her.

"Robin and Olivia, welcome! So sorry I'm late, I was manifestly delayed," she explained.

"It's okay …" began Olivia, smiling kindly down at her. The old woman took her hand and shook it warmly. She stared up into Olivia's eyes and gave a knowing smile.

"This is a blessing," she announced, with a strange sort of affection. "I am very glad, not only to have come, but to have met you both."

She took Robin's hand next and shook it with the same friendliness.

"I've been working long and hard to uncover what's going on, but I regret to say I've drawn a blank so far. However, with your help I know we can find out the truth of this together," she declared, with vigour and determination etched on her face.

"There is tea downstairs," prompted Peter, leading the way. As she left, Olivia noticed a book, which for some reason she couldn't help but take with her. The book was entitled *Chronicles of Barnet – Legacy of the Tomlinsons*. She didn't notice as Robin took one last furtive glance at the sword before departing.

They all returned to the north living room and resumed the conversation. Kat listened as Olivia enlightened them, with no small amount of feverishness, about the situation. Olivia couldn't explain why she felt so pleased Kat was there. There was an affinity between them, like two old friends, though that was impossible as they'd never met before.

"Jack Tomlinson is dead and has named you as beneficiaries in his will," surmised Kat, sipping her tea delicately. She coughed but recovered quickly. "And clearly we've no idea why."

"*Legally declared* dead," Robin reminded her, with significance. "Not quite the same thing."

"Babe!" Olivia chided, hoping he hadn't inadvertently affronted anyone.

"No, no, he's right," said Kat, dismissively. "However, we have to assume that he *has* passed. Truth be told, even if he is still alive, he'd have a hard time preventing us." Peter let out a laugh at that.

"He'd try anyway," he said, and Kat gave a wry grin.

"Until next week we don't really know what to do other than wait. It's the will reading then, and once that's done, we will know where we stand. The instructions around this, I'm told, were very thorough," Olivia said with a grin. "Feels like we're dealing with a state secret."

"That's not out of the question; the Tomlinson line did interact with royalty on more than one occasion," Peter pointed out in a serious tone. "And more than one generation were in the military." Instead of dismissing that as wild speculation of the most unlikely variety, Kat just nodded. Robin and Olivia looked at one another. This family had secrets … or, this family *has* secrets?

# CHAPTER FIVE

# Dear Darkest Solitude

# Unawake

How twilight slides away and falls into the night is one of the most subtle occurrences known to all. The last vestiges of light tumble away silently, surrendering all to the darkness. The stars, there all the time of course, become visible, as does the moon. Tomlinson Hall had seen many such nights which did not make those inside feel secure, safe or sheltered. In fact, it made them feel decidedly uncomfortable.

Robin and Olivia were surprised when Kat and Peter both departed just before darkness descended. Kat even said something about no one having stayed there overnight since the mid-eighties. Robin, Olivia and Fido had the place to themselves.

"There are no hotels nearby," said Olivia, lightly. She always tried to hide when she was scared by speaking with jollity.

"It's not so bad," he said, rubbing her back tenderly. "No hotel could provide a bed like this anyway." They stared at the king-sized four poster bed that Peter had prepared after they'd confirmed they'd be staying. Olivia had to admit he was right about that.

"I just … this place," she tried to explain, words failing her. She waved her hands helplessly.

"I mean… they trust us with all this."

"A lot of it isn't the sort of stuff someone could just run away with, but we both know we'd never find our way out of the village," he said, trying to be funny.

"Okay, which side do you want?" she asked, nodding towards the bed.

"You choose," he beckoned.

"No, I can't make my mind up," she sighed.

"I'll take the left ..."

"Then I'm closest to the door," she said, nodding towards it.

"I'll take the right ..."

"And so I get the window?" she asked, annoyed.

Robin thought about it, gave up, picked her up amid her surprised protest and hurled her onto the bed.

"Right it is!" he laughed as she bashed him with the pillow repeatedly.

Afterward, they lay cuddling in the darkness.

"I love you," she whispered.

"I love me too," he grinned, squeezing her. "I love you."

They were just drifting off when Olivia stiffened.

"Babe!" she hissed. "Did you hear that?" Robin sighed, having heard nothing.

"No," he grumbled, nuzzling against her ear. "Go to sleep." Silence ... he could tell she wasn't going to let it go.

"Please, babe!" she squeaked, fearfully. Knowing it was no use to argue, he slipped free of her and, pulling on his dressing gown, approached the door.

He inched it open, listening hard, fully expecting to hear nothing. Something brushed past his leg, making him shriek in terror, and the light came on as Olivia hit the switch. Fido leapt onto the bed and started licking her. Robin swore under his breath. All she'd heard was Fido pottering around and now, after nearly fifteen minutes of trying to get him to leave them in peace, he'd scammed his way back in. Deciding to just give up and live with the giant furry hot water bottle that liked to crush his feet all night long, he was about to close the door when he heard something else.

Fido, too, reacted by freezing and facing the door. Ironically, this time, Olivia was the one who'd heard nothing. It had been a tapping noise, just a single lone tap in an unfamiliar place, so not 'pinpointable'. As much as he wanted to shrug it off as the Hall itself making sounds, he decided to investigate. Olivia and Fido followed him outside into the corridor. They stood there in silence.

"What?" she asked at last. She was much happier with Fido there and pleased that he wasn't going mental – this meant, to her at least, that they were not in any real danger.

It took nearly twenty minutes to cover the entire Hall, but they found no one and nothing. The sound Robin had heard was unidentifiable. It was a spooky experience, wandering around the Hall in almost total darkness, but a big dog could make you feel surprisingly brave.

"We just need to get used to this place and its sounds," Robin whispered into Olivia's ear. Even he was feeling oddly better that Fido was there. Olivia sighed, and they both climbed back into bed and drifted into sleep. The Hall was in darkness and only the ticking of the clocks made any noise – the silence was otherwise stifling. The portraits that were hung along the stairway stared out as if in waiting. The grandfather clock chimed every hour of the night, the ceaseless ticking and the back and forth of the pendulum continuing even with no one there to perceive them. Or at least there shouldn't have been anyone there …

The sun regained supremacy as it rose the next morning, emerging from behind the tree line, all ethereal and bright. Olivia was in the kitchen, trying to find the toaster. She'd not been up long and was fiddling with the loaf of bread when she turned and nearly screamed the place down as she bumped into Robin.

"Morning," he yawned, completely unaware of her reaction. Fido's nose came up, nearly dislodging her plate.

"Fido!" she hissed, annoyed.

"I'll take him out," said Robin, helpfully. Doggo had to do his business, like anyone, after all. When the front door closed, Olivia was struck by the clocks and the stillness.

She was a grown woman! She should not be afraid to stay in a house with a big dog for four days! She shivered, nonetheless. She couldn't put her finger on a word to describe the hall. 'Creepy' seemed a little mean, but it was hardly a 'normal' environment. Robin would drive back to London after lunch, she knew, and would not return until Friday evening after work.

"Just seventy-two hours, give or take," she assured herself, in an undertone. They'd been apart longer than that, obviously, but not like this. She knew that she mustn't tell Robin she didn't want him to go, as he would say that she had wanted the trip in the first place and that she was trying to make him feel bad. He had enough on his plate, what with his job and everything.

She slowly ate her toast while flicking through the book she'd taken from the library the day before. Fido trotted back in and the front door closed noisily. Robin made that 'brrr' noise he always did when reacting to the cold, and came in rubbing his hands together.

"Crisp one out there today," he stated conversationally. "What's that you've got?" She showed him. "So, after lecturing me about the sword, you half inch a book, eh? Nice." She pulled a face.

"I'll put it back," she declared, rolling her eyes playfully. "I–" The doorbell clanged and they both started. Fido, tail wagging, vanished back out into the entrance hall.

"It's Peter!" called Peter through the letterbox. Robin and Olivia shared a glance. Robin opened the door and Peter was assaulted by the dog, but coped well enough.

"Down, Fido!" commanded Robin and was surprised at Fido obeying. He'd been so much more obedient lately … why didn't that seem true to form?

"Not to worry," chuckled Peter. "How was your evening?"

"Pleasant enough," shrugged Robin, deciding against mentioning the odd noises and other assorted, unexplainable phenomena. He knew the man was the caretaker so he would surely know about all that. Then again, Peter may never have stayed overnight. He'd said no one had since the eighties, and both he and Kat hadn't hung around when it started to get dark …

*No, no, stop that!* Robin reined himself in. He was being ridiculous! What was he thinking exactly? That the place was haunted or something? He didn't even believe in any of that gobbledygook and hadn't since he was a child! He was just about to deploy the mother of all clichés, the one about old wives' tales only told to frighten the children into obedience when, mercifully, another thought struck him. So, too, did Olivia as he'd been so deep in thought, he'd unintentionally ignored her question.

"What?" he blurted in surprise.

"I asked a question," she stated, in long suffering tones. "What time are you setting off?"

Robin thought about it as he had the previous evening, calculating the time it would take and what time the rush hours were. Well, rush day, if he was being honest: London never stopped. For some reason that last notion made him feel exhausted.

"About four," he settled on. "Yes, four."

"Marvellous, lunch *for* four and you leave *at* four, that's very easy to remember," jested Peter, pottering around already.

"I was thinking we could take Fido out to the village?" suggested Olivia, anxious to learn more about Albany-on-Lea. Peter halted in his tracks as if frozen by an epiphany of vast and foreboding proportions. As Mick the farmer had done, Robin thought Peter might warn them against doing that. Though Mick hadn't really warned them, not exactly, but he had certainly inferred that it would be best to avoid the pub and, now they knew a bit more about why they were there, Robin was starting to see why. Instead, Peter gave a little shrug to himself after thinking it over.

"That's good, yes, the church is particularly nice," he said, scratching his head. "Heavens, is that the time? I've just remembered I've got to trim that bush outside. Lunch will be around one." He began to scuttle away.

"I think there might be trouble at t'mill," sighed Olivia after he'd gone.

"Maybe – no one will say anything though, right?" he asked, frowning. "I know this is a village and not London, but we've got Fido."

"If we're right about this being ... awkward," she said, taking time to settle on the word. "Then I think that's why Peter brought up the church. He's sending us somewhere he thinks we won't get into trouble."

"Trouble," echoed Robin, grimly. "Maybe we should just stay here ..."

"No! I don't want to stay in all week and this is my only time to go out with you and Fido," she argued. "Please, Robin?"

The rasp of a bush cutter began loudly. They looked at one

another, neither wishing to sit through that for long. In a few minutes they were being pulled along the road by Fido who was excitedly tugging on the lead.

"It is nice here," she said, holding onto Robin's arm as usual. "You don't get birdsong like this in London."

"No, they much prefer *Bohemian Rhapsody*," he mused dryly.

"Are you going to be in this mood all day?" she queried with a little smile. He immediately burst into song with a dramatic impression of Freddie Mercury, and she laughed.

Father Clapton stared at the new gravestone with a faint smile. The earth, freshly dug, was no longer in the shadow of the church behind him. Decorated all around with colourful flowers, which he personally tended to, the Church of St Nicholas stood out in the village, easily the loftiest structure. Yesterday morning, that grave had been open and empty but now, even though it was full of earth, it was empty of remains. He looked up into the wispy clouds far above in search of the dark clouds he knew had to be gathering somewhere. He smiled as he thought about the Almighty looking down upon the village. Some barking got his attention and he watched as Robin and Olivia appeared on the road.

"There they are," he murmured to himself. He turned and walked back into the church.

"It's an impressive church for a village this size. Didn't get a close look at it yesterday," Olivia was saying.

"I think it's bigger than we thought it was; I mean, it's got a school somewhere so that implies a certain population level, that's if it's still open," rambled Robin. Now that they weren't in the car, they could see a lot more cottages than they had on the way through the previous day. They entered the churchyard and began to head towards the door, Fido tugging furiously on his lead. He wanted to run around like in the park at home, but there was no way he was getting off the lead this time! either of them noticed the faces in the windows of the pub opposite, watching them.

The Old New Inn had been the only pub in Albany-on-Lea since the seventeenth century. Established 1653 by an officer in the Parliamentary army and, curiously, a surviving Cavalier nobleman, working in concert. Hence the sign being that of a metal helmet and fascinator, resting on a red flag with a blue and white cross. It was a symbol of the end of the war and the flag was a combination of the opposing flags in the conflict. The front of the pub was decorated by multiple flower displays and, in the fifties, they'd gone for a Tudor revival look, tall white walls with black wooden beams.

Inside, it was more of a Victorian feel with frosted glass, booths and two fireplaces. It was furnished with comfortable chairs and bar stools, and multiple menu boards with artistic chalk depictions. Maisy Bisbrown polished a pint glass distractedly. She was the landlady and the one responsible for not only the chalk art, but the flower displays too.

"What can you see?" she growled, hating herself for asking. Twenty-odd people were crowded by the window and had been there since Timothy Williams had spied the new arrivals. Unmoved, Mick hadn't shifted from his spot in the corner. But then he'd already met them though he hadn't told anyone about it. Not only would hardly anyone listen to him, but he didn't fancy playing centre stage to an inquisition – not again.

"They have a dog," replied Agatha King, straining on her tiptoes to see.

"Why are they going to church this late?" asked Andy King, puzzled. Since the funeral the previous morning, it had been all everyone was talking about: the four beneficiaries of Jack Tomlinson's will and who they would be. It was a mask for the real question: *who would get the Hall itself?* Once Robin and Olivia were out of sight, Andy returned to his chair and stroked his narrow pointy beard thoughtfully. His wife Agatha joined him seconds later.

"I don't think I can wait a whole week," she grumbled.

"No choice," he replied, tetchy as always.

"That was the definition of anticlimactic," smirked Maisy, amused at their disappointed reactions. What did they expect would happen? "Not seen you all so sad since the World Cup."

"This affects all of us, Maisy, even you. If things go south for us, they'll go south for you," warned Andy, glaring up at her. Maisy only shrugged, infuriating him further. There hadn't been a fight at that pub for over ten years, and it had been between Andy and the head of the Williams family, Sam. Sam had been at the window and was now sitting with his wife at the furthest table from Andy and Agatha.

Maisy had first come to Albany-on-Lea in 2007 and, until the arrival in 2020 of the young couple from somewhere in Kent, Jake and Toggle, she was the newest inhabitant of the village. Something that some of the locals, the Kings mainly, never let her forget. Being landlady of the only pub, however, she was soon able to find her feet and figure out her new clientele. Born in Dagenham in the 1960s, Maisy had worked in pubs her entire life. First, she'd been worked as a barmaid, and gradually she'd worked her way to the top. Before coming to Albany-on-Lea she'd turned down a job with the brewery. A social butterfly, Maisy had learned how to fit in with anyone and, more intriguingly, how to get them to talk. Regarding this matter, however, she'd not have to try very hard to discover more about the two newcomers.

The church, large and echoey, made their every footstep seem impolitely loud. Robin and Olivia took in the interior without a word. It had a very churchy feel, which some might say was appropriate. Candles were flickering and their light made a golden eagle lectern gleam majestically.

"Quiet, isn't it?" breathed Robin in her ear. She squirmed a little and giggled.

"Yup," she agreed. They approached the nearest wall and started to read the plaques, stained glass, and stone carvings. They heard the sound of approaching footsteps as Edmund advanced towards them. Fido sat there, watchful but unbothered.

"*In the world you will have tribulation. But take heart; I have overcome the world.* John 16:33," smiled Edmund, clasping his hands together.

"My name's Robin and that's not the time," replied Robin, confused.

"It's from the Bible," muttered Olivia, smiling. "Hi." She introduced herself, and they all shook hands and paws.

"It is rare for us to have visitors here," stated Edmund, taking a small step back. "Let me know if you need anything …" He had to speak loudly not to be obscured by the drinking sounds coming from Fido, who was availing himself of the silver dog bowl the church provided.

"Actually," said Olivia, looking up at Robin quickly. "We were wondering if you could tell us more about this."

"What?" asked Edmund, though he knew what she was talking about.

"The village, the church, everything," replied Robin, trying to appear casual. "We're strangers here." Olivia cringed at the cliché, but Edmund seemed unmoved.

"Well, this church is St Nicholas, and is built on the remains of its predecessor which Henry VIII decided to flatten … after looting it, of course," he said, easily.

"The Reformation," nodded Olivia, pleased that she'd taken more than a passing interest in the Tudors back in her school days.

"Indeed," he nodded. "Since then, it's remained largely

unchanged. My name is Edmund Clapton and I've been the vicar here since my father passed back in 1990."

"I'm sorry," said Robin, cumbersomely.

"Don't be, the job is not difficult," he responded dryly. He grinned fully to show them he was joking. Awkward laugher began.

"So, about Tomlinson Hall …?" began Olivia. They were trying not to look too interested.

"Ah yes, the Hall … would you like to see the Tomlinsons' graves?" he offered casually. "They're all outside in the walled-off area." Robin and Olivia looked at one another. Olivia pushed her glasses up her nose, starting to feel intrigued. Paintings were one thing, but gravestones were another thing.

Outside, just as Father Clapton had told them, were the Tomlinsons, from Edward all the way through to Jack. Robin pointed when he saw it and Olivia gasped.

"Jack …! But there's no body?" she blurted, quite forgetting to try and keep up the act.

"That's right, we buried a casket yesterday morning before the storm," he explained.

"But … is that normal?" she queried, puzzled. Why bury an empty coffin?

"No, not exactly but there is no rule against it, not when it's the desire of the deceased," he remarked.

"But …" Robin stopped himself. They'd come for answers and were only getting more questions.

"So, these are all the Tomlinsons," sighed Olivia, impressed.

"All but one," Edmund corrected her. "There is another, buried on the opposite side of the graveyard."

"That's … why's that?" she asked, not sure what to think.

"Come with me, it's the grave of Edward, the sixth generation. He passed in 1985. I was here for the funeral; indeed, it was the last burial my father presided over." Father Clapton led them along the narrow paths between the graves and the flowerbeds until they came to an unkempt looking tombstone. On it read: *Here lies Edward Tomlinson 1946 – 1985*. Compared with the other Tomlinson graves, it was strangely bereft of detail. They listed children, spouses and even had messages and quotations on them, but Edward's was bare.

"Only thirty-nine?" noted Olivia, her tone one of reverent curiosity.

"Yes, you'd probably be best asking Peter for the details, he did know them quite well, after all," replied Edmund, artfully.

"Did he?" asked Robin, knowing a game was being played. It was the kind of game where just knowing it was being played was not enough, as the rules were still indistinguishable. That wasn't to say that if you knew the rules it would be much help either as, he was sure, it was a teams-based game.

"He showed us a picture of the brothers as children," ventured Olivia, becoming more standoffish.

"It was a long time ago," said Edmund, in a reflective tone. He gazed into the middle-distance as he remembered. It had been a rainy day when that casket had been bequeathed to the earth. There had been a lot more people living in the village back then … he feared that Albany-on-Lea was dying. Even his own son had moved away after the death of his wife. The Kings and Williams families too had lost others to the lure of London. Edmund really couldn't say if anyone would still be there in fifty years. He didn't resent the modern world as he understood and accepted that change was inevitable, but the sadness clung to him. *The end of an era*, as the phrase had it or, on the other hand, the start of something else.

"We are a unique village here at Albany," said Edmund, breaking the silence. "Since the beginning of the last century, and arguably before that, we've been made up primarily of four families. The Kings, the Williamses, the Claptons and, as you know, the Tomlinsons. It's clear to me but not to many others, that the time of those four families has passed. Tomlinson Hall is key to the survival of this whole village." He paused and looked, as they stared at him evaluatively. "If you want to talk more, you can usually find me here," he said, moving away from them. "Take care."

"What the hell was that?" asked Olivia, deep in thought.

"Language," cautioned Robin, motioning at the graves. Olivia looked down at them self-consciously.

"Sorry," she apologised, in a pantomime whisper.

"I said it last night and I'm saying it again, what have we walked into here?" he growled.

"Obviously, the Hall is hotly contested; I think he was trying to warn us subtly," she suggested.

"Everyone's been trying to warn us about one thing or another since we arrived," he complained, rolling his eyes. "I wish someone would just say whatever it is in plain English."

"Maybe they can't," she protested, shrugging. Robin glanced at his phone.

"We'd better get back, I need to make sure the car is okay," he said, remembering he needed to check his tyres and fuel before heading back.

# CHAPTER SIX

## Dear Darkest Solitude

## Sleepless

Notes from *Chronicles of Barnet – Legacy of the Tomlinsons* by Professor of History Tracey Stannett MSc (1961-2014)

*Let's dispense with the notion that the Tomlinsons were a family of squeaky-clean reputation. They were not. Edward Tomlinson was rumoured to have been a member of the infamous Hellfire Club, or one of its variants, and some even believe it was Edward himself who stole a certain urn from West Wycombe. As a wealthy industrialist, it's unclear where he came from or how he rose to such prominence; however, it is evident that he had personal dealings with both George III and George IV. Functions were held at Tomlinson Hall around the 1810s with some regularity. It's the consensus of leading experts that Edward came from Ireland, but this is not confirmed.*

*From 1834 to 1835, Rupert Tomlinson (1803-1878), brother of Henry Tomlinson and youngest son of Edward, spent time in jail on charges of forgery. There are two main theories as to how he escaped his ten-year sentence. The first was that his brother Henry pulled some strings to get him released early. The second was that direct intervention from King William IV occurred after Henry's wife, Gwendoline, petitioned him for help.*

*The wealth and fortune of the Tomlinsons is still a hotly debated topic, as is Rupert's contribution to it. Some suggest that Rupert could have been the* legendary Spring-heeled Jack, but I have found no evidence to support that. Rupert was purported to have unusually good luck; but the way I look at it is, lucky as he was to be released early from prison, if he was that lucky he'd never have been caught in the first place.

Now we've covered the black sheep of the family, let's move on to the mysterious disappearance of Lucy Brown (1895). Lucy was a labourer for most of her short life. We believe she was born around 1870 but it's not definite. She came to work at Tomlinson Hall around 1893 but wasn't seen again after April 1895. The leading theory is that Arthur Tomlinson was having an affair with her and, when she became pregnant, he had her murdered. The second is that Arthur and Lucy were having an affair or Suzanna Tomlinson, Arthur's wife, believed they were, and she had the girl removed. Again, common theme here, but there is no evidence to say one way or another for sure or, come to that, even if she was murdered at all. One thing everyone agrees on is that Lucy was never seen again.

The meal was divine; Peter was an unexpectedly skilled chef. Mostly, the conversation had been around Robin explaining to Kat and Peter where he worked and what had happened regarding his employment status. Warming to his theme, Robin regaled them on what he and Arnie had been discussing regarding their options. Fundamentally, it came down to a situation best compared to The Clash song *Should I Stay or Should I Go?* Little did Robin and Olivia know, but Kat and Peter found the situation or, at least, Robin's take on it, ironic. After all, from their point of view, they had similar feelings when it came to Robin and Olivia's continued presence at Tomlinson Hall.

"Sounds like a lot of pressure," said Kat after a brief coughing fit. "I would be all at sea these days, no idea what I would do."

"Are you okay?" asked Olivia, a bit concerned. Kat gave her a warm smile.

"Lungs are not what they were dear, twenty a day habit back in the day saw to that," she explained, with a throaty laugh. Robin frowned as he watched the old woman pour herself a tiny glass of tequila. He was avoiding the wine as he was driving but Olivia, unusually, asked for a shot of her own. Peter was having a red wine but had put the bottle back on the sideboard, implying that it was only going to be for him.

"Now," smiled Robin, trying to make this sound like he was half joking. "Can I trust you two to keep my girlfriend out of mischief while I'm gone?"

"No," stated Kat, immediately. Olivia covered her mouth as she giggled.

"Just checking," he said with a half-smile.

"What do you think I'm going to do? Have a party?" she jested.

"No idea what you and Fido get up to when I'm not there," he replied. He put his hand on hers to let her know that he was being somewhat serious.

"We'll be fine, I'll call you every day like normal," she promised. "I'll not disappear, like Lucy."

"Lucy?" asked Kat, eyeing Olivia in surprise. "How did you find out about that?" Sheepishly, Olivia slid the book across the table.

"I'm sorry that I borrowed this without asking, but …"

"Goodness me!" gasped Kat, flicking through the book. She seemed fascinated. Peter too appeared to be watching with great interest.

"Not seen this book for years, thought it was lost," she elaborated. She looked up at the ceiling for a moment and shook her head as if in admonishment. Robin raised an eyebrow as he looked up as well, but saw nothing.

"The Hall must like you to show you so much so quickly," Kat declared, returning the book to Olivia. Olivia smiled uneasily.

"The Hall?" she asked; she wasn't sure she wanted to know.

"Oh yes, this place has a ... sort of character, or disposition," explained Kat, animated now. Robin and Peter made eye contact; Peter merely shrugged. "It decides who it likes and who it doesn't. That's what Maria Hayden seemed to think when she visited in 1853." Olivia hurriedly googled that as she had no idea who she was and, after reading Wikipedia for a few seconds, she gaped.

"You know, I do have to sleep here *alone*," Olivia reminded her, tepid trepidation tinging her tone.

"Don't worry, you'll be fine," said Kat, reassuringly. "No one's seen anything untoward here since the eighties."

"That might be because no one's been here," pointed out Peter, unhelpfully. He cleared his throat. "I mean, Kat's perfectly right, there's no documented ghost sightings here."

Much later, outside the Hall, in the drive, Robin was reassuring Olivia.

"You'll be okay," he said, hugging her tightly. "You're sure the signal is good here? If you have trouble connecting, I can come back to get you."

Olivia was a graphic designer who also helped create websites. Indeed, her interest in art had been partly how she'd met Robin in the first place. They had first encountered one another aged eight when he ruined one of her drawings. It had been her latest attempt at a fluffle of rabbits and, though she said so herself, was the best drawing she'd ever done. Her mother used to read her Peter the Rabbit a lot when she was younger, hence her devotion to the carrot-munching monsters. She'd even owned one in her teens called Archimedes, a white rabbit with a black spot over his left eye and a mild salad addiction.

Anyway, the drawing … she'd been planning on showing it to the teacher to prove she'd taken in everything he'd told her about shading. Robin had been fighting with the other boys about something completely unrelated, which neither of them could remember now, and had ripped it in two as he fell. She would have told the teacher, only all the other boys said they would back up Robin and say she'd torn it up herself!

It had been an accident, but Olivia had been so incensed that no apology would make a difference. This was followed by a six-month period of all-out war where they would fight and prank one another mercilessly. Both had endured their first and several other detentions due to the machinations of the other. All that had changed when one day he found her crying and somehow, they settled their differences. From then on, they became a team who gradually morphed into close friends. As teenagers it was clear to everyone but them that they were meant for each other. Then, at age 17, they began dating and had been together ever since.

He was waving at her from the car, and this last sighting of Olivia and Fido standing outside the Hall together was meaningful, not in an overly jarring way, but more like a subtle, mental occurrence which only happens some time afterward, like a repressed memory finally reaching the end of its time, locked away under a charge of behaving in an overly traumatic manner. Robin would later place this moment in the spot usually occupied by the calm before the storm.

He'd always found the expression 'turning lives upside down' to be slightly moronic. Not only did it presuppose that said life was right-side-up in the first place, but as it neither caused time to fold back on itself or reverse ageing, it was entirely inaccurate. Nevertheless, logic aside, their lives were about to be jostled violently, to such an extent that it would result in a profound change in direction.

The drive back to London was uneventful. No unusual weather, no eerie songs, and he didn't even get lost. Indeed, though he was driving towards his problems, he was oddly aware that he could be driving away from them.

As soon as the car was out of sight, Olivia had suddenly felt very alone. She cuddled Fido as she considered her situation and faced the Hall.

"Just three days and some hours," she said to herself. The building seemed to be looming over her oppressively. Taking a deep breath, she went back inside and joined Peter and Kat in the north living room. There was a feeling that she'd just interrupted a conversation, but the idea of spending the night in the Hall all by herself was distracting her. Fido being there was very reassuring, especially as he had been much more obedient lately.

"He'll be back soon enough," smiled Kat, kindly. Olivia smiled weakly in response.

It was late when Robin finally reached the flat. Traffic jam on the M25. Without Olivia and Fido, the flat seemed colder, somehow … that, and the central heating was off. He remembered to send her a tender text, letting her know he'd got home safety and wishing her a good night. Robin thought he'd left the days of microwave meals for one behind, but apparently not. Still, there was a lot to be said for wolfing down a lukewarm plastic-encased lasagne on an empty stomach. By God, he knew how to live. Next, he caught up on Netflix, then endured a lightning shower, and finally, during the first few pages of a book, Robin felt sleep tugging on his jugular, thereafter repositioning on his eyelids, and soon he fell into a deep sleep.

He opened his eyes, suddenly wide awake. The room was as dark as it had been when he'd fallen asleep. He found that he couldn't move. Now, Robin had never experienced sleep-paralysis before, but he naturally assumed that that was what he was going through. He became distracted, however, when he noticed a dark shape on the chair in the corner. Despite telling himself multiple times that it wasn't a person and that this was all some kind of nightmare that he'd no doubt awake from, his eyes were becoming more accustomed. It was a man!

Robin couldn't call for help, couldn't get up and fight or run; he could only stare at the man in the chair. The fear was palpable, but disbelief still hammered out a powerful counter argument through his heartbeat. You're dreaming! This isn't real! If it was real and this was an actual intruder, why is he just sitting there? The longer he stared, the more he could make out; indeed, he would later reflect on just how much he could see. It was as if the man in the chair had a faint glow that made him that much more visible. It was at this stage that Robin, at last, recognised the face. He'd never met this man before, yet he'd seen that face!

A blue-blooded, refined, stern face with eyes that seemed unable to decide if they were dark amber or brown. Where had Robin seen this man …? Then he remembered and, with a jolt, he sat up, mouth agape as he stared at what could only be Edward Tomlinson. That proved it! It had to be that he was unable to escape a sleep-ridden reverie. How else would it be possible to see a man who'd been dead for nearly two hundred years? What might have been a knowing smile flashed across Edward's face, as if he was reading Robin's thoughts (which, of course, he easily could if he really was a figment!).

"What do you want?" was the only possible utterance for Robin. Edward did not answer but maintained eye contact. A sense of reassurance washed over Robin. If Edward, assuming he was real, meant him harm, he surely would have struck already? That didn't tell Robin why Edward should come to him, though. It had to mean something, right? He doubted that Edward was the sole representative of the obscure hobby of sleep spectator. Robin finally managed to stand, and approached the chair slowly. When he reached out and his hand went straight through Edward, he initially felt relieved. Yes, this was a dream, fantastic, all he had to do now was wait until he woke up. No one slept forever, after all.

The cold rush of air that travelled up his arm and gave him goosebumps, however, was not so encouraging. Edward seemed unmoved by the contact and just continued to sit there, now staring up at him, that same forbidding glare that Robin had seen in his portrait on the stairs. At last, in a deep gravelly voice, Edward finally spoke. It was one word, and it was said in such a way that it made Robin wonder if he'd meant it in a good way – or not.

"Welcome."

Robin sat up again, only just able to contain his own shriek. He was back in bed, and panting heavily and sweating, he looked all around. The room was dark, the chair was empty, and everything seemed normal. After calming down, he fetched himself a glass of water before returning to bed. While he was quite warm and comfortable, sleep eluded him for the rest of the night. He kept looking at that chair, expecting Edward to reappear at any moment, but he didn't, of course. How could he? Nothing had ever been there really; it was just his own mind misfiring. Right?

That same night, back at Tomlinson Hall, Olivia restlessly tossed and turned in the vast bed. She was not used to sleeping alone and had been creeped out when Peter and Kat had, once again, despite her mild protestations, vacated the property shortly before darkness fell. Why did they have to keep doing that? She'd been very relieved to read Robin's text and had sent kisses back. Now, as she lay there, she badly wanted to FaceTime him but knew he'd be asleep as he needed to be up early. Trying to relax, she rolled onto her back and felt the furry mound next to her shift slightly. Fido had wasted no time in taking Robin's place next to her. As she lay there, staring up at the ceiling, she thought she heard something. A faint tap-tap sound. Sighing with annoyance, she slipped from under the covers and pulled on her dressing gown.

Using her phone as a torch, she edged out into the passageway beyond. There it was again, a little louder now. She halted, her nerves kicking in. Surely she and Fido were alone? The dog would have gone nuts if anyone else was there! The tapping was coming from one of the other bedrooms. She pushed the door all the way open and froze in absolute horror. The rocking chair was moving! It was shifting ever so slightly back and forth as if someone had just got up from it. She backed up against the wall, covering her mouth to silence her own involuntary whimper.

Then, when she saw why it was moving, she slid down the wall into a relieved sitting position. The curtain was under the chair and the window was open. The intermittent breeze was causing the curtain to pull on the chair. She let out a laugh and shook her head at herself. She walked over, eased the curtain free from the chair and then closed the window. She flashed the iPhone around the room one last time, just to make sure all was in order, before promptly returning to bed. She slept soundly the rest of the night and, while she was making toast the next morning, Peter returned.

Even though he had a set of keys for everything, he knocked to allow her to let him in, which was very respectful of him.

"How was your evening?" he asked politely.

"It was fine," she smiled, easily. Then she remembered her little scare but decided against telling him about it. She was feeling somewhat annoyed with herself for reacting like that and wasn't going to admit to it if she could help it.

"I thought you closed and locked all the windows before leaving?" she queried, subtly.

"That's right," he nodded, unsuspecting.

"I'm not sure you …" she began, when he spoke again.

"Ah, drat, I do apologise," he said, hurrying away. She thought he was going to run upstairs and close it and was about to tell him she'd already done that, when it became apparent that he was not going upstairs at all. He instead went to the lower guest bedroom and closed a window in there. He returned, shaking his head.

"My fault entirely," he said, shaking his head. "In my haste to leave yesterday I overlooked it."

"So, you only left one window open?" she asked, suddenly concerned.

"Yes."

How had the other window been left open if Peter hadn't opened it?

"Peter, why do you and Kat never stay here overnight?" she asked, directly. He smiled as if it was the easiest question to answer.

"Never have," he stated as if it was obvious. "Indeed, you and Robin are the only two people to have spent the night here since the eighties."

"Yes, so you said, but you never said why," she persisted, trying not to sound too bothered.

"Well," he said, pausing and then shrugging. "It just wouldn't be right."

Later, while she worked on the website for a client, Olivia decided to have a little break. She'd taken Fido on a short walk that morning but only around the gardens. These were extensive and all of them backed up on woodland. It wasn't long enough for Fido, she knew, but after nearly getting ripped from her feet twice, she'd decided to return to the Hall.

She sat in her chair, slowly stirring tea that Peter had, very generously, made for her without her asking for it. She didn't mean to, but she began to daydream. The scent of flowers came to her out of nowhere, but it wasn't like actual flowers, it was more like …

"Caron Bellodgia perfume, rose, jasmine and musk," a woman's whispery voice said. Olivia inhaled deeply and lounged back in the chair. Her eyes closed and then an explosion of music made her open them again in surprise. Her laptop was playing by itself! She leapt up to turn it off but halted when she saw what was playing. The Charleston. Another wave of that perfume hit her and then next thing she knew, she was dancing. She stared down at her feet, grinning as if intoxicated, watching as her fluffy pink slippers morphed into dancing shoes. Olivia would later realise that not only could she not dance but she certainly couldn't dance like that.

In that moment, however, it was like she was at a party and everyone around her was doing the same thing. Long dresses swirled, glasses clinked, and laughter sounded. She managed to look up and stare into another woman's face. Her smile was warm, but her eyes were sad. Olivia instantly knew who it had to be – Anne Tomlinson. She looked much younger here than in her portrait, but she was unmistakeable. Was she hallucinating or something? She wanted to show Robin how she could move, and started to seek him out even though she knew he wasn't there. It all stopped suddenly, and Anne leaned in to whisper once more.

"Party."

Olivia leapt up off her chair in reaction and nearly spilt her tea. Peter came in at that moment, carrying a pile of clothes. He'd explained that one of his responsibilities was to ensure nothing was damaged and that included moth deterrent.

"Is everything all right in here?" he called, over the music. Olivia switched it off.

"Yes ..." she said, unconvincingly. He regarded her for a moment in silence. She studied what he was carrying and gasped in shock as she pointed to the garment he was holding. It was a very familiar looking sequinned shoulder cape – the one Anne had been wearing! That was weird! *So* weird!

"Would you like to have this?" he asked, offering it to her.

"I shouldn't," she said, almost snatching it from him. Carefully she put it on and stared at herself in the mirror. Peter looked on, a little hesitant. "This … is great," she managed, suddenly on the edge of tears. "Who …?"

"Anne Tomlinson," he said, confirming her suspicions. "It belonged to Anne, and she would sometimes wear it at social gatherings." "And when she danced," she stated as if she knew. How the hell did she know that? He smiled uneasily.

"And when she danced," he repeated, a little perplexed.

Olivia stared at herself in the mirror, wearing the garment. It seemed to fit her perfectly. Just for a moment, she thought Anne's face appeared over hers. She snapped out of her trance and looked all around.

"Sorry, I was daydreaming," she admitted, laughing awkwardly. "Thank you for the tea."

"You're welcome," he said, bowing his head. "Will there be anything else?"

"I have no idea," she breathed, her mind taking flight once more.

"Call me if you need anything," he said, backing out of the room. Olivia briefly refocused on the mirror before managing to return to her laptop. She really must get on!

News bulletin: Arni offered to buy a pint and the nation was dumbfounded. There are some events which just happen after a terrible day, the news being broadcast, for example. A stiff drink, something of ancient origins, was another prominent and even pertinent specimen.

"We're screwed," Arni had said, between slurps. Robin had been suffering all day due to his bad night, but at that moment nothing was further from his mind than either of the Edward Tomlinsons. Indeed, he was so distracted, he'd not answered Olivia's texts. Unable to focus, guided more by routine than actual purpose, Robin had practically sleepwalked his way through the day. However, he had finally managed to take in how monumentally bad their situation was.

"I just don't see how things could have got this bad without anyone twigging," sighed Robin, gutted. "There's no chance?"

"No," Arni groaned.

"Get anywhere with your applications?"

"Not yet, you?"

"No," said Robin. They just sat there, staring into their drinks, oblivious to the clatter of the bar around them.

"Doesn't feel like a Tuesday," noted Arni, almost absently.

"There's always tomorrow," said Robin, rising from his chair. That most probably wouldn't feel like a Wednesday.

Still feeling only half awake, Robin made his way home. He knew he should text Olivia back and speak to her, but he didn't have the energy. It was all he could do to grab some dinner, shower, and then crawl into bed. Asleep in moments, Robin had decided to sort everything out in the morning. Sadly, he was due for another rude awakening. As before, he awoke, initially unable to move. He looked over to the chair, expecting Edward Tomlinson to have returned. To his surprise, though, the chair was empty. For a moment, he almost relaxed – until he noticed the tall figure looming in the doorway.

It was a man, tall, broad and, by all appearances, cloaked. He brandished a sword, a sword that Robin had seen before. This time there was no build-up, no warning, the man just lunged at him. Somehow Robin rolled off the bed, crashing to the floor and snatching up the baseball bat he kept by Olivia's side of the bed. He rose to his feet, spinning with the bat as he turned. The figure stepped back, and his hood fell away, revealing Rupert Tomlinson. His face was impassive, almost devoid of emotion, and except for his intensely gleaming eyes, he could have been his own portrait! Indeed, he sort of was …

For a few frantic seconds, the pair fought, though it should be worth noting that apparently neither of them could reach the other. The fracas, while chaotic and startling, did astonishingly little damage. Robin would later realise that the only bruises he had – on his elbow and knee – were, arguably, self-inflicted when he fell off the bed. Seeking an escape route to the hallway, he froze in his tracks as Rupert vanished into thin air. Blinking blearily and staggering around, Robin accidentally decapitated the standard lamp. He hit the floor with a groan and became conscious of a loud thumping from next door.

"Shut that noise up!"

"Sorry!" called Robin, still panting.

*It was as the bullets whistled by overhead, and I hunkered down harder, and the freezing sea wind cut into my flesh, that the thought came to me. Quite by chance, as revenge was the last thing on my mind at that moment. I knew it was over, there was no chance to regroup, my brother had made it impossible. Without knowing where it was all hidden, despite years of searching, I knew my only option was to temporise. Delaying the inevitable, others would infer with their usual trite smugness. My only regret is that I must leave her behind.*

Kat put down the book slowly, its worn pages flicking closed in the breeze. Olivia, pulled along by Fido, was approaching her. They were in the garden outside Tomlinson Hall.

"Morning!" called Olivia, waving as she got close. Kat smiled, recognising Anne's clothing instantly.

"Good morning, Olivia, you're looking very vivacious and bushy tailed," said Kat, patting Fido gently. His tongue lolled free of his jaws as he panted heavily. "Peter will be out soon with some herbal tea for me. Would you like some?"

"Thanks, I may look it, but I don't feel all that wonderful. Yes, tea, why not?" Olivia replied, taking a seat opposite the old woman. "What were you reading?"

"Oh ... nothing important," sighed Kat, sliding the battered looking book away. "What's the matter?" It seemed weird that Kat should be the one for Olivia to confide in – normally, she would have turned to her best friend, Maria, or her mother, but Kat seemed so wise and personable.

"It's Robin, he's not answered any of my texts. I've not heard from him since he got ..." she stopped before saying the word 'home'. She glanced back at the Hall, not even sure why the word didn't seem right suddenly.

"You both told me he's trying to save his career. I'm sure he'll be in touch as soon as he can," Kat said, reassuringly. It had been Monday night when he'd last texted her, and it was now Wednesday late morning. From what she could tell, he'd read her messages but not answered.

"He is under a lot of stress," she allowed, trying not to let the hurt get to her. Changing the subject, Olivia brought out the book she'd been avidly reading. *Chronicles of Barnet – Legacy of the Tomlinsons*.

"Did you know Anne Tomlinson well?" she asked, hoping she might have. Kat was about to answer when Peter arrived.

"Ladies," he addressed them, setting the silver tray neatly on the table before them. "Twinings, Orange and Cinnamon Spice."

"You're a walking miracle, Peter," smiled Kat, appreciatively.

"Thanks," replied Olivia. When Peter had returned inside, Olivia tried again.

"Father Clapton told us a little about what happened between Edward and Jack. That must have been hard for Anne to deal with, especially after Henry's passing?" Kat poured the tea slowly.

"Ah, I remember being young and so full of questions too," she said, softly. "Look, Peter's brought milk even though we don't need any with this." She chuckled and shook her head. "Always stuck in routines is Peter, dependable as a grandfather clock." Olivia's smile wilted a little at the change in subject – perhaps Kat didn't want to talk about it.

"Anne was like two completely different women in one body. She could be very formal, cold and even rude at times. Yet at parties she held nothing back," explained Kat.

"She liked to dance?" guessed Olivia, not that it was much of a guess at this point.

"It was one of her principles to dance with everyone present, both men and women," chuckled Kat, remembering. "Even us kids were not safe. I never knew anyone with as much energy. Then again, maybe that's why outside of the parties she was so still and stoic. Only Henry could charm a smile out of her if she wasn't willing to give them out for free. Then … you know what they call the war generation?" Olivia shook her head. "The Greatest Generation."

"So far," Olivia added, in an undertone. Kat heard and smiled.

"Yes … so far. Very well said," she agreed, toasting her. Olivia gently tapped her own cup against Kat's, pleased she'd not offended her.

"Anne would have loved you," went on Kat, out of nowhere. "I believe she was so strict because of Suzanna. When Anne first met Henry, I'm not sure Suzanna took to her at first so she might have created that persona to deal with her mother-in-law. She was over ten years younger than Henry, after all, and Suzanna could be very overprotective of her little boy. When Suzanna died, maybe she kept up the act to help her through the war, and, afterwards … well, old habits die hard."

Kat's smile faded. "Say what you like about Suzanna, hard as nails she might have been, but she didn't see the end of the Tomlinson line. Anne did."

"It began with an Edward and ended with one," noted Olivia, in comprehension. "But Jack was the last …" Kat didn't seem to hear her.

"It was a long slow fall from grace. Edward was out of control, whittling away the family fortune until there was nothing left," sighed Kat, genuinely regretful. "Everyone tried to stop him. Henry tried, Jack tried more than once, Anne and I tried … I'd never seen someone so hellbent on lunacy before. It was frightening."

"How did Edward die?" asked Olivia.

"Death certificate said overdose," she replied, sadly. She shook her head before taking another sip of tea.

"So, you could say Edward had more in common with Rupert, whereas Jack was more like Henry?" asked Olivia, thinking she was getting somewhere. Kat looked at her, beaming.

"You really are doing your research, aren't you?" It was true that Olivia had hardly put that book down.

"I thought someone had better do some," she replied, raising an eyebrow. She tapped her phone screen with her fingernail with significance. "Others are apparently too busy to be troubled with it."

Kat pulled a face. "I think Robin cares an awful lot about you, that's why he's fighting for his job so hard," she said. "He'll reach out to you soon enough, you'll see."

"I wish I had your patience," responded Olivia, with a sigh of her own.

"Why don't you take your mind off it and give that dog some exercise, visit Father Clapton? He'd like that and, who knows, you might learn more," suggested Kat, trying to rally Olivia. The younger woman nodded.

"Yes, I will," she replied, standing up. "Come on, Fido, just don't go nuts, all right?"

"Olivia!" called Kat, casually. "You might meet other people from the village on your way. Try to listen prudently to what they have to say, be polite, but remember that some things are best not taken at face value." Olivia wanted to ask more but Robin's lack of communication was still distracting her so, instead of pressing for more details, she just nodded and let Fido take the lead (that is to say: go first, not actually take his own lead - that would be a recipe for fruitcake).

This not sleeping thing was starting to get to Robin. After being attacked by someone who wasn't there, he'd been afraid to answer the door, never knowing who might be on the other side. Turned out it was his next-door neighbour, just passing by to ask if everything was okay. With one look at Robin's dishevelled and unshaven appearance, it should have been abundantly clear from the offset that things were very much not okay. Then again, it was London, and the fact that he interacted with his neighbours at all was a miracle.

After making it to just after five in the morning without sleep, paranoid about another nightmare, Robin had fallen asleep just before his alarm went off. He checked his phone out of habit to see that more increasingly affronted messages from Olivia had arrived. One even had a frowny face and no kisses! That was serious. Indeed, seriously, it was hard to put into words just how seriously serious that was. Reprimanding himself inwardly for having forgotten to contact her since the evening before last, he swiftly started reading them.

He was about to reply when he spotted a more urgent one from Arni asking him where he was. Robin was now seriously late for work. Barely six hours of sleep in over forty-eight, he was starting to struggle now. On the positive side, at least he'd not wet the bed yet. The unnerving truth was that he was more worried about what would happen that evening, when he tried to sleep again, than he was about the ticking off he'd get for showing up late to the office.

"What happened to you?" asked Arni, shocked, when they met in the office.

"I was attacked by a long-dead forger," Robin mumbled as he slurped his coffee. Arni frowned.

"Seriously mate, you're not looking yourself …"

"Then who am I looking like …?"

"Come to that, you weren't exactly on fire yesterday either. There's a mental health helpline to call," he continued. Robin just continued to drink as if he was very thirsty, but the truth was he was after the sugar and caffeine. Anything to stay awake!

What was he even doing there? The injudicious notion of just walking out, driving back to Tomlinson Hall and not even looking back entered his mind.

Attempting such a journey on that little sleep was foolish, he knew; exhaustion could indeed kill. He had no desire to go the same way Primrose had. The idea of leaving all this behind, however, wasn't without some basic appeal. Was this all his life had become? A cog in a machine, endlessly rotating until one day the fuel ran out! He looked around the office with a sudden dislike. People he couldn't care less about taking up his time, affecting his life, contributing to a premature decline of career. He'd believed them at school and college, the teachers and vocational advisors, when they'd told him that a career was the most important thing – the be all and end all. Even his parents … had they all lied? Robin couldn't tell if he was thinking straight – he needed to escape this crushing vice that he'd allowed his life to become.

Somehow, clinging to the waking world, Robin managed to endure the tediousness and futility otherwise known as the working day. Dead on his feet, he marched through his own graveyard shift, unable to summon the enthusiasm required for clock watching. When, at last, it was time to leave, he didn't even join Arni and the others down the local for more scheming. He knew he probably should in case anything new had developed, but he was too weary to face anything. He didn't remember the journey back to the flat, having made it somehow on autopilot. His last act before flopping back onto the bed was to remove his shoes. Things were so bad, he'd forgotten dinner …

Edmund looked up from what he was reading – a set list proposal from the local children's choir – when he heard footsteps in the lobby. Fido tugged his mistress along with all the delicacy he could muster, so not much. Honestly, it seemed he must have been a husky in a previous life. Olivia, a little red faced and breathless from the run (no journey with Fido could be described as a jaunty walk), smiled.

"Hi, me again," she said, struggling with the lead.

"Ah," he responded, fending off Fido's enthusiastic advances.

"Down!" she instructed, firmly. Fido sat down, tail thumping the floor loudly, his salivation glands dampened by the last of the morning dew.

"How can I help you, Miss Higgins?" he asked, though he already could guess.

"It's about the will reading in two days' time," she explained, a little nervous. She still hadn't quite decided what to ask. "Will you be there?"

"Practically the whole village will be," he shrugged with a little chortle. He'd been questioned extensively by many of the villagers about Robin and Olivia by now. Luckily, he'd always been good at dodging questions – an essential skill for a member of the clergy.

"Robin and I, and Kat obviously, are all beneficiaries of this will but … it mentions …" she paused to unfold the codicil. "Robin, his wife/partner … as two of the four beneficiaries." She jabbed at the text with her fingertip before pushing her glasses back up her nose.

"Right..." he nodded, not knowing where she was going with that.

"Well, on Kat's codicil, it just says her name ... so that's three ... do we know who the fourth is?" she asked, curiously.

"Not from this, no," he replied, reading it casually. "I suppose we'll find out at the reading."

"Also, I might sound a bit insecure but ... Robin and Kat are both named, I'm just wife/partner," she elaborated. "Do you think that might be because whoever wrote this, wrote it at a time before I was with Robin?"

"Well, yes – I mean, Jack disappeared in the mid-eighties so ..."

"Yes, but that predates Robin's birth, too, so there's no way Jack could have known either of us, which means he didn't write this?" she went on, rather excited.

"Well, obviously Jack must still have been alive after 1985, and I understand you were both born in 1990?" he confirmed, and she nodded. "I believe the last sighting of Jack was 2010 in Paris, but that's not definite." She shook her head. "Believe me, his connection to either of you is a mystery to me too, but I'm sure we will learn more at the reading."

"Doesn't it bother you, though?" she asked, in a pantomime whisper. "Kat is the only one of the beneficiaries you know. Robin and I are not just strangers to you but very removed from all of this. We'd never even heard of Tomlinson Hall two weeks ago."

He laughed and held up his hands. "All I can say is, we have to wait for the reading, unless you're prepared to try and wheedle it out of the solicitors," he repeated. She sighed, letting that go for now – the lawyers had to remain silent in accordance with the will itself, apparently. "It's hardly a surprise to me. You, as you have pointed out, didn't know Jack. For those who did, this mystery is not unexpected. He was a very private man."

"Private enough to have complete strangers brought in on something so personal?" she frowned, not sure what this meant.

"It seems so," he nodded, unruffled.

She sighed and sat down on the pew. Edmund occupied the one in front of her and sat side-on so that he could still face her.

"You've done this sort of thing before, right? Wills and death, and like … stuff?"

"And taxes too," he chortled. She didn't understand the reference.

"Are they all like this?" she demanded, frustrated. He pondered that for a moment and stared up into the beautiful rafters.

"No," he stated, at last returning his attention to her. "Indeed, I've never encountered one so different."

"Great," she breathed, rolling her eyes. "Someone, somewhere, that's still alive, must know what's really going on."

"Well …" he paused, and then gave her a warm smile. "Can you keep a secret?" She leaned forward intently.

"Of course."

"So can they," he grinned. She slumped back with a groan. "Perhaps you should ask yourself why Jack felt the need to make things the way they are?"

"What do you think I've been doing?" she growled, checking her phone again. Still nothing from Robin. She shot off a rude and demanding text without really thinking.

"The answers you seek could be at the Hall itself," he hinted cryptically.

"What, you mean in the library?" she frowned. She loved that place, she really did, but the idea of searching through all those books gave her a bit of a headache. She could only cope with one book at a time; if she tried more that that she often ended up confusing them.

"Surely Peter or Kat have mentioned the lost treasure?" he asked, a bit more softly. Her eyes went wide.

"No ... they must have forgotten that bit," she remarked, not too sure about this.

"They must have at least told you who Edward Tomlinson was?" he asked, a bit annoyed now.

"Well, they said he was an industrialist." she recalled.

"A very wealthy one," he replied. "No one really knows how he acquired his wealth, but we know that he didn't spend it all on the Hall. We also know that Rupert, the conniving skinflint, added considerably to said fortune with his own ill-gotten gains."

"Yes, but then the last Edward Tomlinson lost all he could find in the company of Lord Lucan and his ilk, that's why Jack disowned him," she argued, confused.

"All he could find," echoed Edmund, with significance.

"So, you think there's other money Jack hid from him?" she asked, allowing her scepticism to show. "That won't be at the Hall; that, if it exists, would probably be in a bank account or shares somewhere."

"Possibly," he acknowledged. "Assuming it's money in the conventional sense."

"But Edward is dead! Who is Jack trying to hide it from?" she demanded, crossly.

"Again, you're assuming he found it," he replied, standing with a groan. Before walking away, he looked at her one last time. "I suggest you have a good rummage through the whole Hall, you never know what you might find."

Robin sat up, wide awake. By now it was almost like routine, and he knew what was coming. There was a man in a suit, sitting in the armchair in the corner. Henry Tomlinson was unmistakable and unchanged from his portrait back at the Hall. He smiled openly across at Robin who sat there, panting with adrenalin.

"Henry?" asked Robin at last. Asking who he was would have been silly as he already knew that, and demanding to know why he was there, as if he were an intruder, seemed rather rude.

"Yes," nodded Henry, proudly. "Yes, I am Henry." Robin activated the video on his phone and tried to record the apparition, but it only showed the chair and darkness. Henry just continued to smile patiently as if all this was a game.

"You came to me for a reason, you all did, say it," ordered Robin, a bit fiercely. In truth, he was still frightened but at least Henry wasn't carrying a sword.

"Now I like that, succinct and direct," said Henry, his eyes gleaming. "My family and I have been visiting you and your beloved to find out who our replacements are." It took Robin a second to dissect that answer.

"Replacements?" he echoed, dwelling on the word. Then another came to him, and his eyes flashed. "Olivia? You've been attacking her too?"

"Rupert goes his own way, he always did," dismissed Henry, uninterested. "Don't let it all go, don't leave it to them."

"What are you talking about? What have you done to Olivia?" he demanded, not really listening anymore. Henry, though, was fading slowly away. Robin fumbled for his phone and, without checking his messages, called Olivia. He would later realise how pointless this was as not only was she furious with him for not answering her texts, but it was also the middle of the night!

"Don't leave it to them," repeated Henry as he vanished completely.

"Henry!" hissed Robin, remembering to keep the noise down this time. "Don't leave what to whom?"

He tried to call Olivia again but with the same result. Great! Now he couldn't sleep again! It was one extreme to the other. Sighing, he decided to leave it until tomorrow; he'd see her when he got there, and she'd know he'd at least tried to call her.

# CHAPTER SEVEN

# I, Jack Tomlinson,

# a Resident of Albany-on-Lea …

The phone vibrated loudly on the table. Fido looked on as Olivia stared at it in a trance-like state. In the mirror there was a woman standing behind her but, outside of the reflection, there was no one there. Olivia knew who this woman was: Suzanna Tomlinson. Even if she didn't recognise her from her portrait, the full skirt and intricately braided golden hair made her identity obvious. Slowly, Suzanna extended her arm to place her hand onto Olivia's shoulder. One silver ring occupied her fourth finger. Olivia felt cold all over as if someone had tripped over her grave, in the dark, while searching for their missing pooch, whom they couldn't find, due to being fatigued from a long battle over custody.

In the mirror their eyes found each other. There was something important Olivia had to do, very important. Suzanna never said a word, but conveyed all her meaning through changing expressions at incredible speed. Indeed, one would have to be on speed to do that so quickly. It was like speeded up footage with a scratchy white noise in the background. In a sudden wave of apprehensive awareness, Olivia broke free and swung around, arm defensively lashing out at nothing. Panting, she looked around and freaked out when she heard something rolling across the floor.

Fido leapt from the bed and sniffed inquisitively at the bronze bracelet that had come to rest by Olivia's foot. Gently, Olivia crouched and retrieved it. Holding it up to the light, she was struck by its simplicity. Engraved along it were four letters and it took Olivia all of two seconds to know what they stood for. ATSW. Arthur Tomlinson and Suzanna Williams. This had been a gift from Arthur to Suzanna when they had been sweethearts and now Suzanna was passing it on to her. After hesitating for a moment, Olivia slid it onto her arm and regarded it curiously. It felt right. In the mirror she took in her appearance, wearing Anne's shoulder cape and Suzanna's bracelet. Competing thoughts jousted in her mind but were quickly forced to stop on health and safety grounds. These notions were: *this is so weird,* and *this is so right.*

She took her phone, now silent once more, dismissed the missed calls from Robin, and activated the torch.

"Come on," she said to Fido. She led the way into the corridor. "Edmund said to search this place and I might need a sniffer dog." Fido, presumably thinking they were going in search of food, trotted gamely along beside her. She peeked into the library after theatrically shushing him for no reason. They entered and she cast the light from her phone around the room. Then she closed her eyes. She was being stupid! She turned the light on like a normal human being.

It was all as it had been before. The books, the relics, and the decorations.

"Did he mean just search the books, or literally search the Hall?" she murmured, to Fido. Her eyes went wide as they both heard a door downstairs slam shut. Fido barked and took off running for the stairs. Olivia followed, taking care to not trip in her slippers. She didn't want to fall over anything while chasing her own dog. Fido continued to bark, and sat himself outside the door to the cellar.

"Who's there?" she called, more interested than scared. No answer. She opened the door and Fido slid inside.

Again, she turned on the light and stared as Fido snuffled around a wall towards the back. Edging past the mostly empty racks and crates, Olivia had to use the light on her phone again as it was still dark in the corners. There was nothing to see. Just cobwebs and old white bricks. A black wooden beam was nailed up with four hooks on it. She gripped each one in turn, acting on instinct. She tried to manipulate them, get them to turn or slide. All of them remained uncooperatively rigged. Fido looked up at her.

"I wish you could talk," she said, seriously. Frowning, she gripped the beam in its entirety and pulled.

To her surprise, it slid forward a good inch and a half. She let out a gasp as part of the wall silently eased back. Darkness was beyond. Fido, for once, stayed put. A secret passageway! No manor house in England could do without one. She paused, debating her options. There was no way she could sleep, knowing this was here, without at least exploring some of it. She had a big dog with her so she wasn't too concerned about safety, but she was worried it might lock them inside. She grabbed one of the crates and wedged it under the wall to stop it from shifting back.

Once she'd got in, she realised she needn't have worried. A lever conveniently labelled 'Close' was right there. The passageway was both higher and broader than she thought it would be. Their way lit only by her phone, they padded into the musty smelling darkness. Robin was never going to believe this! Had Edmund known this was here? Did Peter? They walked on and on for a surprisingly long distance. It had to be a few hundred metres and still no end was in sight. On the positive side, they didn't find any offshoots or rooms, so she wasn't concerned about getting lost in some underground warren. She had, after all, forgotten her thread.

She halted with a sigh. Rationally, she knew it couldn't go on forever, but then neither could she.

"We'll wait for Robin and then, assuming he's still talking to me, we'll figure this out," she stated to Fido. "We won't tell anyone else about this," she went on as they hurried back.

"Someone's using this to get in and out of the Hall and I don't know about you, but I don't think it's a ghost." Fido heartily agreed. "I wonder what they want ... obviously not us." That was the thing, she didn't feel threatened at all. Spooked, maybe, but she most certainly wasn't in fear of her life. If anything, she felt more concerned about the village than she did about the Hall. She would go there the next day and see what else she could uncover.

Robin blundered into the office, having overslept again. Arni frowned at him.

"Where were you last night?" he demanded crossly.

"I'm sorry... Olivia ..." he blethered, with a 'what can you do' shrug. Olivia always found it funny how many things he blamed on her to his colleagues. *Can't go to that party because my girlfriend wants me home. Can't attend that conference as my girlfriend wants me home.* Even Fido was fair game these days. *Can't do this as my dog gets lonely. Can't drink too much as I need to be able to walk the dog.* Oh yes, and, *Can I take the remainder of that bone home with me?*

"Forget it, I don't want to know," retorted Arni, rolling his eyes. "Listen, there's a light at the end of the tunnel."

"Can you see it's the end?" asked Robin, amused.

"What?"

"Well, I mean, it might just be a light in a tunnel, one of many, there to light the way, but how do you know it's at the end?" he qualified, slapping the computer for slowness.

"It's nice to see you're a bit more yourself today," he remarked, levelly. "I was explaining to Erica last night in the pub that an old pal of mine is setting up a company and he needs people he can trust.

Your name was bandied around."

Robin grinned, exultation rising in him. The joy passed like a diverted train at Clapham Junction, brimming with indifferent self-importance and smug detachment. Robin found himself deflating in much the same way as a birthday balloon, as if the occasion itself had filled him and, now that it was over, he leaked purpose rather than air. After all, in its way, every day was the anniversary of your life. Instead of falling from said hypothetical platform onto the rails of despair, Robin instead felt conflicted. He was at a junction and its name was very much *not* Clapham. There had been a shift in the points, and he couldn't read the destination.

"Do you have the details?" he asked suddenly. Arni was a bit nonplussed by this response but nodded.

"I've sent them to you," he said.

"When do you need to know by?"

"As soon as possible, but ideally now," Arni replied.

"Sorry, I have things to consider," explained Robin, trying to elucidate what he did not yet know.

"Well, yes, we all do, that's why we're doing this." Arni leaned in close before continuing in an undertone. "Staying here is not an option, mate, it's this or the dole queue."

"I know, it's all very important. But I need to go," he replied, standing up. Arni frowned.

"Long lunch appointment, is it?" he asked, sceptically.

"I need to … I …" he frowned. He had to talk to Olivia about this. It wasn't just the career now; it was something else even more imperative. Arni was regarding him evaluatively.

"Maybe you should take the rest of the day off, mate, you're looking awful," he said, crossing his arms.

"Thanks," Robin said, hastening away as if hunted by the hounds of hell.

Making it back to the apartment in record time, due to avoiding the rush hour that could no longer be contained within an hour, Robin stood there, motionless. He then slowly walked around the place he'd once called home. It had seemed so significant, so central to his life ... well, their lives. Why was living in London so important? Why was living anywhere so vital to so many definitions of successful? Everyone knew achievement didn't guarantee happiness, even if the two were intrinsically linked. How much of his life had he lived for other people, or because the narratives of the times dictated that he did as such? Now, he could spend the rest of his days asking himself rhetorical questions if he liked, but he sensed it wouldn't get him very far.

He glanced at himself in the mirror and recoiled instinctively. Beard growth had struck once again during his period of absentmindedness, and he rubbed his stubble ponderously. Age did creep up on you but, in the mirror, it had to stay still. Again, he looked around the flat, his mind grasping at fleeting memories. The truth was that this place had never really felt like a home. How could it? They were only renting, after all. As if guided by unseen forces or, perhaps, because he wanted to, Robin began to pack his bags. This was not his home and the woman he loved was not there, a lose-lose situation.

Still mulling over her discovery of the previous night, fearless with Fido, Olivia walked down the road towards the village once more. his time, while exercising Fido, she planned to stroll around the village and see more of it. She'd donned another of Anne's capes that she'd found and, not sure why, she'd kept Suzanna's bracelet on her wrist too. They felt like talismans that bolstered her against what she might encounter. Even if she ignored Kat, Peter and Edmund, her own senses were warning her to tread carefully in the village. Despite the unease, she walked with her head held high, her step confident as if she was not alone. On the contrary, beside Fido, she felt like she had two ghosts following in her wake. Robin was never going to believe any of this … if he ever spoke to her again, that is.

Passing the church, she stopped by the war memorial and studied the names on the plaque. It was for both world wars, listing the dates in order. The names were twenty something in total which was a lot for a small village. The Kings, the Williamses, the Claptons, the Smiths, and a single Tomlinson, Georgina. Sighing, Olivia slowly reached out to touch the letters delicately, before lowering her hand and stepping back. Why had Georgina not made herself known to Olivia as Anne and Suzanna had? Perhaps she would …

"Hello!" said a woman, breaking into Olivia's solemn thoughts. Instead of jumping in surprise as she once would have, Olivia turned slowly and almost imperiously to face this stranger. Fido remained where he was sitting and didn't seem bothered by her presence.

"Hello," replied Olivia, with a cautious smile. She took in the other woman, her senior by possibly as much as thirty years.

"My name is Agatha," she said, with a little half laugh.

"Agatha King," nodded Olivia, instantly knowing who this woman was. She'd listened hard to every word Kat had said, and read much of the history of the village by now; besides, perhaps in a previous life they might have met before.

Agatha was, needless to say, shocked at Olivia's knowledge and confidence.

"I'm Olivia Higgins," she smiled, her smile becoming wider. She extended her hand and Agatha hesitantly shook it. "This village is lovely; you must be very proud to live here." Again, Agatha hesitated before replying. This was not how she'd envisioned the conversation going at all.

"Yes, it is rather nice, isn't it?" she grinned. She was not only wondering about what kind of person Olivia was, more than she had been before, but she had an unnerving feeling that they had met before. There was something familiar about her ... which, of course, was ridiculous! They'd only just met; Olivia had just, intentionally or not, got into her head.

"And because we like to be considered nice, I was wondering if you would like me to show you around?" offered Agatha. "It will only take about fifteen minutes. After we're finished, we could go to the pub, and I'll introduce you to those who are in there."

"That would be very nice of you, please lead on," she replied, with a wave of her arm.

Agatha did and, while describing the roads and cottages ably, she did her best to question Olivia about her origins. Where had she come from? Why was she here? How long was she intending to stay? With a verbal agility that surprised even herself, Olivia was able to fend these off with vague responses, ranging from the banal *it depends* to the evasive *you'd have to ask Robin about that*.

Maisy looked up eagerly as the door opened. The event that the village and, by proxy, her pub, had expected had finally happened. Agatha, looking rather flustered – mainly due to her inability to get anything of significance out of the other woman – led Olivia and Fido straight into the Old New Inn. Everyone did a very poor job of pretending to look uninterested, with the exception of Jake and Toggle who were oblivious to the situation. Barking ensued briefly as Fido and a small black boxer dog exchanged greetings. One word from Olivia, though, and Fido went quiet. Maisy looked at the younger woman and saw something she didn't often see in one so young: a blend of confidence, wisdom, and wariness. This one would be a slippery customer, she knew – always fun.

"Morning!" breathed Agatha, all full of faux jollity as ever. "Two teas, please."

"Will that be cups or pots?" grunted Maisy, acting neutral.

"The usual, please," huffed Agatha, not prepared for the odd response. "This is a new arrival, Olivia Higgins from London." Olivia and Maisy stared at one another somewhat standoffishly. The boxer dog, her boxer dog, a tiny little fellow by the name of Fluffy, continued to bark. Maisy shushed him.

"Welcome to Albany-on-Lea and welcome to the Old New Inn," she said, with a welcoming smile.

"Olivia's staying up at the Hall," went on Agatha, a bit excitable. "Isn't that right?"

"For now," answered Olivia. "I was walking around the village and Agatha was kind enough to give me a tour. Magnificent place, I have to say." Maisy was not taken in by this – she knew caution when she saw it. Olivia would be anxious not to offend but she clearly didn't have any issues with being the centre of attention either. Who would be the first to bring up the funeral, she wondered?

Andy approached, a slimy smile on his lips, hand extended.

"Ah, this is my husband …" began Agatha. Before she could finish, however, Olivia completed the sentence.

"Andy King," said Olivia, shaking his hand. She was glad she was wearing gloves.

"How do you know?" asked Agatha. Maisy paid keen interest to this as it was unforeseen. Had Olivia been here before?

"Did you not tell me?" asked Olivia, as if perplexed. "Surely you must have mentioned your husband to me. How else could I have known?" Maisy concealed her grin. Oh yes, this was going to be juicy. Stumped, Agatha had to surrender; politeness dictated it.

"Yes, I suppose I must have," she said, tittering uncertainly.

"You're here for the reading of the will, aren't you?" asked Andy, directly.

"I was listed as one of the beneficiaries," responded Olivia, not quite answering the question. She had been expecting this – something had warned her, somehow, she knew. These people wanted the Hall for themselves. She wasn't sure why, but she just knew they did – just as she knew she mustn't let them take it.

"Did you know Jack well?" she asked before Andy could ask anything else.

After about half an hour of awkward discussion, Olivia was able to extract herself from the pub. In the time she'd been there she'd met what felt like the whole village. She'd encountered the King family, the Williams family, and a few others. From her study of the history of the place, she knew that the Kings and Williamses were two of the oldest families in the village, and had been at times linked to the Tomlinsons through marriage. The first Mary Tomlinson and Suzanna had been Williamses and the second Mary had been a King. Olivia suspected that these marriages would be used to stake claim to the estate.

She'd received a surprising early text from Robin telling her that he loved her and was coming back. She'd not answered, to see how he liked being ignored. Some would say she was being childish, and she would agree, but that didn't stop her doing it. Of course, there emerged the fear of what she would feel like if he died and she'd ignored him? She countered that with the argument that if she texted him now, she might well distract him from the road and cause his death, so she was not answering. Indeed, she wasn't just not answering: she had a game plan.

She reached the Hall and smiled at Peter and Kat when she found them.

"Afternoon," she said. "When Robin gets here, would you mind telling him that I'm not well and he can't disturb me in our room?" Peter frowned and Kat rolled her eyes.

"Certainly, will you require a doctor's note?" asked Kat cynically. Olivia grinned.

"No, not that sick, just sick enough to prevent him from talking to me," she said. She let Fido off his lead, and he padded over to his bed.

"The will reading is tomorrow," pointed out Peter, sounding concerned. "I was hoping we could all talk about it before then?"

"Yes, it's at eleven thirty," Olivia reminded him, grandly. "There will be time in the morning to talk about it." With that she turned, made to grab at a non-existent skirt, and then jogged lightly up the stairs. Peter and Kat exchanged a look and Kat gave a careless wave of her hand before standing with a groan.

"Young love," she chuckled with dismissive fondness.

"Don't worry, you just leave Robin to me," he replied sarcastically.

"Nonsense, Robin's a nice lad, let him annoy her," retorted Kat. "They'll get through it soon enough, I'm sure."

"If you say so."

Robin arrived just as twilight was going through the motions of pretending it wasn't the night's sleeper agent. Peter greeted him and helped him with his bags.

"Where's Olivia?" was obviously the first question Robin asked.

"She's gone to bed, not feeling too well," he replied awkwardly. He gave Robin a meaningful look to convey what that actually meant. Robin let out an impatient sigh.

"Should have replied," he muttered, waving his phone around.

"You look like you've had a few other things on your plate," shrugged Peter. "I've set up a spare room if she doesn't let you in I'll see myself out."

Robin went upstairs and reached the bedroom door. He tried to open it but found it locked so he knocked softly.

"Olivia, it's me, how are you feeling?" he asked, trying to sound tender. He did care and love her and all that, but this was a bit on the irritating side. No answer came.

"You're going to have to come out eventually," he said, conversationally. Olivia was sitting on the other side of the door, positioned so that her shadow didn't give her away. Fido whined and she glared at him. "I heard that, Fido," he said, his voice a bit muffled. "She locked you in with her, did she? You have my deepest sympathy."

Incensed, Olivia replied before she could stop herself.

"We're not talking to you," she said, then covered her mouth, annoyed at herself.

"Then who are you talking to?" his legendary comeback sounded. "Don't tell me you've been visited by ghosts, too?"

"I have a headache so just … what do you mean, ghosts?" she demanded crossly.

"Nothing," he grumbled, wishing he'd not brought it up. "Can you let me in?"

"I can," was her stuffy response.

"Will you?" he groaned with a sigh.

"No," she said, flatly. "By *ghosting* me, you've treated me badly and my feelings are hurt."

"I'm sorry, I didn't mean to ignore you," he growled, thumping the door softly again. "And I did respond eventually but you never answered."

"Only because you never texted me back." Even Olivia was starting to see how silly it all was at this point. She rolled her eyes and opened the door. Smiling, Robin went in for a hug, but she slid away.

"I've not forgiven you yet," she announced snootily. "I am not heartless, however, so, as an olive branch …" She was interrupted as he grabbed and kissed her. She wrapped her arms around him, and it was some time before they stopped.

"I'm sorry," he said, seriously. "And I mean it." They stared into each other's eyes for a moment and a great stillness descended as inner defences crumbled.

"What happened in London?" she asked, sensing he'd been through something. He had already considered how he would answer this question.

"Not sure yet," he brushed off the query. "Arni's got some kind of plan; he always has, but I was questioning my entire career as opposed to the job itself. Started asking myself why living how we were living was so … vital." She paused, curiosity in her face.

"Weird. These last few days I've been questioning a lot of things too," she admitted. She began to tell him about what he'd missed while he'd been away.

"*Curiouser and curiouser, said Alice,*" murmured Robin as he listened. "Don't get me wrong here, I know you've always had backbone, but now it sounds like it's armoured or something." She laughed.

"I don't know, I've been acting strangely, too, lately. Listen, don't laugh, but while you were gone – and don't tell anyone this – I found a secret passageway." The casualness of this disclosure floored Robin for a few seconds and he looked across at her.

"Err, right," he managed after a few minutes, and she giggled at his reaction.

"I'll show you tomorrow," she said. "But we have to be at the will reading in the church so it might be a while before we get to it."

"What's this?" he frowned, running his hand along her arm and touching the bracelet.

"To be honest, I don't know, but I like it so…" she trailed off. She felt his body move ever so slightly. "I found it; I've not spent anything!" she added defensively.

"I didn't say anything!" he protested, annoyed that she'd picked up on that. "Did you hear any words from me about it?"

"No," she conceded, cuddling closer. "But it was the way you didn't say anything."

*

The next day, in the church, in front of the crowd, the suited solicitor looked up and began to read.

"I, Jack Tomlinson, a resident of Albany-on-Lea …"

# CHAPTER EIGHT

## A Church, a Pub and a School

*Note to all readers: You were not there, and, for legal reasons, no one can divulge exactly what the text said. It can be strongly alleged, however, that it heavily covered two serious topics that rhyme with 'honey' and 'precedence'.*

It was quickly established that the fourth beneficiary was present at the reading, but the solicitor was obligated to ensure the name not be disclosed. Olivia had scanned the crowd as this was discussed to see if anyone gave themselves away. Peter seemed unmoved but she was growing more and more convinced that it was, in fact, him. After all, who had been guiding and looking after them since day one? Kat was already a beneficiary so it couldn't be her, and she still claimed not to know who it was.

Frankly, though, the chaos that erupted in the church due to what else the will entailed demoted that topic to little more than an inconvenient detail. Putting it mildly, it was like an overweight lead balloon taking a nose-dive off the end of a short pier. Literally no one got what they wanted or even expected. Well, maybe someone did but, if indeed they did, they wisely kept it to themselves. Robin didn't blame any of them for their reactions and felt distinctly uncomfortable at the side glances and veiled distrust he was perceiving.

Right in the centre of the controversy were Robin, Olivia and Kat, who apparently now owned Tomlinson Hall and, so it seemed, some of the village as well. Peter was now working directly for them as, arguably, was the vicar. Leaving that minor hullabaloo aside, there was also the issue of money. The post office needed to be refurbished and then reopened as apparently whoever owned the Hall, due to some clerical oversight in the 1600s, also supervised the local postal operation. The church roof needed mending, the Hall itself required some repairs and then there were the overheads, the under boards and the side-whiners. It looked rough at the front and had the back end of a blobfish.

Robin and Olivia already knew that the Tomlinson family fortune was gone as that had been the reason why the brothers had feuded in the eighties. Basically, they'd just inherited a vast debt. Owning Tomlinson Hall was not a good thing when you had no money, it turned out. While they wouldn't be paying any rent or a mortgage, they would have energy bills, maintenance costs and a monthly payment to pay back debts to a third party.

To rub salt into the wound, it was quite clear that pretty much the rest of the village resented them owning it. The Kings were particularly vocal. Andy King pretty much summed up the feeling of the room by uttering the obvious question aloud:

"Why them? They're not even from round here!" Olivia went quite pale as she heard the amounts being talked about in terms of bills. She overheard someone muttering that people as young as her and Robin had no business being left in charge of such a property. Based on her lack of experience, she was inclined to agree.

Kat didn't seem remotely put off, however, and perhaps she was the one who had got what she expected. The rest of the village seemed to give Kat a wide birth as if she was not one of them or, that she once had been, but was being punished for some unpardonable indiscretion that could never be overlooked. She also had a similar attitude towards them, barely acknowledging them with even a glance. She stared at the solicitor from under her black hat as if completely unmoved: a large, lumpy boulder facing off against an ocean wave.

"We are quite sure that Jack was of sound mind when he wrote this will, *if* he wrote it …?" asked Sam Williams, looking nonplussed.

"I have been reliably assured that everything here is perfectly legal," was the professional rebuttal from the solicitor.

"This is ridiculous!" declared Andy pompously.

"Now please, let's keep things respectful," warned Edmund, raising his hands diplomatically.

"How did you know Jack?" demanded Enid of Robin and Olivia. Enid was Sam's wife. Neither of them answered, just stood there like statues. They had agreed before they went in not to answer any questions beyond what they were asked by the solicitor.

"How are you going to afford the upkeep?" asked Andy, pushy as ever.

"They don't have to answer that," retorted Peter, showing a more disagreeable persona suddenly. "Shall we go?"

"We need to know what's going to happen with the post office at least!" implored Agatha pathetically. In the midst of the increasingly angry mob, it took everyone a few seconds to realise that Kat had keeled over.

"Oh my God!" cried Olivia, noticing. She, Peter and Robin dashed over to help.

"Don't touch her," warned Robin, seeing that she was pretty much in the recovery position anyway.

Olivia was struggling with her phone to call an ambulance when Kat's hand shot out and grabbed her wrist to stop her.

"Wait," she implored, with significance. Edmund was still forcing the crowd out of the doors. When it slammed shut, a blow that echoed all around the church, he came rushing back.

"You all right?" asked Peter, confused.

"I'm fine," she croaked, with a wink. "Got rid of them though, didn't I?" She started to laugh but instead began to cough, and she groaned as they helped her back onto her chair.

"You're sure you're all right?" asked Olivia for the tenth time.

"It was a trick," she insisted with a wave of her stick. Robin and Olivia exchanged a relieved glance.

"I should have guessed. I'm not sure how God would see such a performance in His own house," remarked Edmund sternly.

"I'll find out soon enough," she answered, unconcerned. "We were never going to get rid of them any other way. Are they waiting outside?"

"I imagine so."

"The back way?" she suggested. "Let's get back to the Hall."

It was after lunch when they were finally able to understand the financial plight they were in. Robin sighed and dropped the pen on the table. Olivia rubbed his shoulder tenderly as they both stared down at the figures. Twenty-one thousand pounds a month in outgoings, plus over three hundred thousand pounds in debt. The only incoming lucre was a monthly payment of ten thousand pounds from an anonymous source. Kat put away her reading glasses and sat there opposite them with her eyes closed. Peter busied himself by polishing the teapot nervously.

"Given that it's been this way since the eighties, I'd say we were lucky the debts aren't higher," murmured Robin with a grim chuckle.

"Anonymous payments have occurred over the years, lowering it from time to time," said Peter.

"You knew about this?" asked Olivia.

"I knew things were bad, but I never questioned it," he replied honestly.

"I can't see a way out of this without help from the bank," sighed Robin dismally. "We can't do anything, we've no money."

"I should have saved more," grunted Kat, shaking her head.

"If things are this bad, why is everyone so upset we got it?" asked Olivia, confused.

"Well, Andy King has the capital to get out of this," said Kat. "Richest man in the village. I don't know about Sam and Timothy, but I'm assuming they do too. That's why I was a bit concerned they were so angry. I thought they would be annoyed at the wait, but no more."

"The wait?" asked Robin anxiously.

"Well, we're going to have to bail on the Hall if we can't sort all this out. We don't want to sell it but neither can we keep it," she explained.

"What about the fourth beneficiary?" asked Olivia, eyeing Peter.

"Even if we knew who it was, what are the odds that they have the disposable income to drag this place up off its knees?" asked Peter, shrugging. "We know it's someone in the village, but it's clearly not one of the Kings or the Williamses, unless someone's a brilliant actor."

"Sadly, it's not just a case of settling the debts and fixing everything, it's got to be maintained afterwards too," Kat reminded them.

"Where is this monthly payment of ten thousand pounds coming from?" asked Robin.

"I never dared ask in case it stopped," replied Peter. It was his wage, partly, so obviously he didn't wish to mess with it.

"HRH," read Olivia, from the payment. "Could be a company. I'll google it."

"Did Jack own any companies?" asked Robin, earnestly. Kat

shook her head.

"Not that I know of. Ed got his hands on the businesses before Jack was aware of the danger. Most were sold off to pay Ed's gambling debts." Robin sighed again, more heavily this time.

"It's weird," said Olivia, still puzzled. She scrolled through the search results sadly. "Logistics … properties …" She cancelled the search, knowing it would be hopeless. It could be a company that dealt with properties.

"And I don't know *what* we're going to do about the school," said Robin, turning his attention back to it.

"Closed since the end of term 1990," noted Kat, with a bittersweet gleam in her eyes. "Mrs McGregor did her best to keep it going but, after five years, mortality struck."

"She was the only teacher?" asked Olivia, only just able to comprehend the idea. She and Robin could count the number of times they'd seen the same teacher twice on one hand. Then again, theirs had been a town school – this seemed to be somewhat different. Indeed, nearly everything about this place was different.

"She was; she taught English, French and Spanish to what was, at the time, called sixth form students – I've no idea how they would be labelled today," she explained. "Lovely woman, loved flowers, children and books. Never married or had any children of her own, so she had a lot of free time to read and to educate." Robin glanced at Olivia but didn't say what he was thinking. Did everyone come to this place to die? Albany-on-Lea was so beguilingly lethal that it claimed victims that didn't even live there anymore. Jack Tomlinson, for example …

"And the owner of Tomlinson Hall now owns the old schoolhouse," Robin reminded them, pointedly. He glanced at the folder on the school and closed his eyes. "And it's got damp." Kat gave a little shrug. It was the least of their worries.

"Shall we take Fido for a walk, clear our heads?" offered Olivia, trying to be subtle. She fooled no one, of course, and Kat gave a knowing smile. Robin rose from the chair, nodding. Fido, the only one who was anything other than depressed, yanked hard on the lead as normal. He led them down the drive excitedly.

"Let's not go through the village," said Olivia. She wasn't frightened of any encounters with anyone, but neither did she wish to invite them. Instead, they turned the other way and found a bridal path that led them through the woods. They trudged along in silence for several minutes, arms linked. The path was overgrown, and, at times, they had to duck underneath low hanging branches.

"Doesn't look like this is well travelled," he remarked, casually.

"What are we going to do?" she asked, unable to hold the question in any longer. "I don't want to surrender the Hall to anyone, but we haven't the cash to save it, and neither have our families."

"I'm thinking," he offered, though there was no hope in his voice.

That was when they came upon a bench. Fido continued to leap about while they read the plaque: 'In memory of Anne Tomlinson'. The rest was too rusty to read. For some reason this brought tears to Olivia's eyes and made her more determined than ever to save the Hall.

"We could get a loan …" she trailed off. That was not going to help at all, even if they could get it.

"If only we knew who the fourth beneficiary was," he grumbled, annoyed at the secrecy.

"Pretty sure it's Peter. If it was someone rich, they would have made themselves known to us by now," she said. "We're paying him right now, technically, so he can't help us."

"Assuming it *is* him …"

"Yes, I am assuming," she argued, irritated. "Who's your money on?"

"We should talk to your father, he might know what to do," he suggested.

"He might tell us to leave and forget it," she retorted. She expected Robin to question why she wasn't willing to do that and was surprised when he didn't. There was nothing wrong with that as a plan if you were divorced from the situation – if you looked at it dispassionately, it was a sensible notion, except that the debt would probably still follow them.

"I don't know why but I really don't want to leave this unsolved," was his delayed response. "It wouldn't be right."

"Same here."

"It's Kat I feel sorry for. I can't in good conscience leave her in the lurch," he went on. "I know she wouldn't blame us, but I would."

"We'd put Peter out of work," she sighed. "Potentially." A deep silence fell between then and even Fido was staring to look downcast. A stiff breeze blew, making the trees whisper and swirl. From somewhere nearby, a crow cawed portentously. Olivia shivered and clung more tightly to Robin's arm.

"This is so strange, all of it," he went on, shaking his head. "Why us?"

"Why you," she corrected, pointedly. "I wasn't named, you were. The link, whatever it is, is to you. Not that I'm trying to get out of this or anything …"

"There is no me, there is only we, so it's, 'Why us?'" he said, kissing the top of her head. "I'm dragging you into this, whether you like it or not."

She laughed. "Okay," she allowed.

"There's always a way." he ventured, tentatively.

"Hope so," she nodded.

Ahead of them, the trees were beginning to clear, and a field was coming into view. A distant rumbling noise reached them, and they stared out across the field, leaning against the old wooden fence. A familiar tractor was approaching them.

"This guy again," noted Olivia, more intrigued than apprehensive.

"Good," sighed Robin, waving to the man. "I've got to ask him something." Olivia already knew what that would be.

"I don't remember seeing him at the reading of the will," she mused.

"No … me neither," he agreed. "Then again, next to us now, he's the biggest economy the village has. If anyone should have been there, it's him."

"Maybe he's the fourth?" she hissed suddenly. "That might explain why he didn't show up because he already knew what would …"

"Afternoon!" hailed Mick as he got close. "Nice to see you two again. Glad you made it to the Hall in the end. It was pouring down that day, wasn't it?" He reached across the fence to shake hands and greet Fido.

"Very wet," agreed Olivia, sociably.

"I think it's safe to say we might never have reached the village without your assistance," smiled Robin.

"No flooding, though, we got away lightly," he smiled, waggling a finger.

"Speaking of getting away lightly …" began Robin, carefully. "Did you know who we were when we arrived?"

Mick's smile dropped a little, but he nodded. "I suspected," he admitted, sighing. "Truth is, I wasn't sure until you told me you were bound for the Hall, and that's when I put two and two together …" He trailed off. "It's also why I did my best to prevent you going into the pub. I figured ... it would be best you avoided that place on your first night here."

"Because of the villagers?" guessed Olivia, remembering her own interactions with them.

"Honestly? Yes."

"You could have warned us less vaguely," pointed out Robin.

"Oh yes, and you'd have believed every word from me, wouldn't you?" he replied dryly. "No, if I suggested anything, it would have been me you distrusted. Besides, at the time, I couldn't be absolutely sure I was right about who you were."

"I don't understand why you chose to warn us at all," said Olivia, perceptively. "Could it be that you had advance warning that we were coming?"

"If you're asking if I am the fourth beneficiary then, with mixed emotions, I can put my hand on my heart and assure you that I am not," he smiled, kindly. Olivia didn't bother to hide her disappointment.

"So how did you know we were coming?" asked Robin.

"Jack Tomlinson had been declared legally dead, so I guessed someone would be turning up at some point – stands to reason. Even if it was the taxman himself and, believe me, I thought it would be. Your appearance took everyone by surprise."

He stared at them evaluatively for a moment before speaking again.

"The truth is, I did have another reason for warning you away," he elaborated. "My name is Mick Williams. Sam is my older brother and Timothy is my younger brother." He held up his hand as Olivia opened her mouth to ask a question. "I'm the black sheep of the family – we hardly exchange greetings these days. Frankly, the idea of either of them getting their hands on the Hall, after what they did to me, seemed appalling."

"What happened?" asked Olivia, as anyone would.

"Ah, I was young and stupid. There was a woman and it all ended horribly. My brothers tried to use the situation to take the farm from me. They'd never forgiven me after father left it all to me. He'd done it, not to spite them, but because I was the only one who knew how to milk the cows."

Robin and Olivia exchanged a glance at that, but continued listening.

"See, they went off to university, which our parents paid for. I stayed and helped my father run the business. While they were enjoying parties and eating brunch, my father and I wrestled with Mother Nature from dawn to dusk. When he became sick, my mother and I tended to him and though Sam and Timothy did visit, they remained aloof – they trusted mother and me to deal with everything. It was their joint assumption that they would reap the benefits, but instead they reaped the true seeds they sowed and got very little. Of course, they both made it, and they out-earn me handsomely today, but that's not helped them get over their resentment. If they had got the farm back then, they would undoubtedly have sold it. Today, if they got the Hall, they would sell that too … they don't care about the survival of the village even though they say they do. If they did, they would understand why Tomlinson Hall needs to be given to someone who loves it."

"Their claim is that Suzanna Tomlinson was once a Williams," said Olivia, flatly. "They see it as theirs."

"And Mary Tomlinson was originally Mary King, so that's why the Kings see it as theirs," argued Mick with a feral grin.

"But the first Mary Tomlinson was also a Williams," responded Olivia, crossing her arms.

"It's ours," stated Robin, firmly. "At least it is for now."

"Until you run out of money," noted Mick levelly. "If I could help you I would, but ..." He pulled a face and they understood.

"Why weren't you at the will reading?" asked Olivia, interested. "Because your brothers were there?"

"Oh no, I bump into them all the time, we just don't say much to each other. No, I didn't go because I knew you would be there. If I had showed my face, you might have asked me these questions in front of everyone and the fact that I knew you were here but had chosen not to tell them could have come out. I never told anyone I'd already met you. I admit I was greatly curious to know how it all turned out, but I figured I'd hear all about it tonight at the pub," he answered. "I'm interested to learn, however, that you don't know who the fourth beneficiary is, but I shall say nothing about it to anyone."

"If you weren't there, how do you know that the fourth is still anonymous?" asked Robin astutely.

"Edmund told me; he often goes for walks through my farm, and we usually catch up when we meet. Indeed, he even speculated that I might see you two around later," he explained. "He gave me quite a lot of detail, actually, said he was worried about you and the future of the village."

"I'm worried about us!" replied Robin, pointing to himself comically.

"Well, I wish you luck, I must leave you now," he said, driving away.

"Wow, this village is on par with social media," muttered Olivia, pushing her glasses up her nose.

"You trust him about not being the fourth beneficiary?" asked Robin.

She shrugged. "I think so. My money is still on Peter," was her conclusion. A distant rumble of thunder shook them out of their reveries, and they glanced at the darkening sky.

"The app didn't mention that," muttered Robin, seriously thinking about deleting it.

"It's like this place doesn't exist," she concurred, nearly stumbling over a log.

They had barely made it through the door as the rain began to hammer down. Peter was there with dinner almost ready, and Kat had already returned to her cottage. Robin and Olivia stared across the long table at one another; it felt odd not sitting next to each other, but it somehow seemed more fitting. The candles that Peter had lit in the centre were pleasing, adding a glow of warmth to the room. Olivia suddenly remembered the secret passageway and couldn't stop a big grin appearing on her face. Robin caught the look and frowned.

"You thought of something?" came his hopeful question.

"I got something to show you later," she whispered critically. The look she got in response made her realise he'd misunderstood. "No! Something about the Hall." He pulled a playfully downcast expression to that, but nodded.

"So, after that – can we?" he asked, reaching across for her hand even though she was miles out of reach.

"Of course," she smiled. "But this could be important."

"I'm off now!" declared Peter, blundering back into the room and startling them. "See you in the morning."

"Yeah, see you!"

"Goodnight, Peter!" Olivia waited until the door was closed and locked before reminding Robin about the secret passageway. What with the will reading and everything else, it had slipped his mind completely.

"Don't you want Peter to know about it?" he asked, poking a thumb over his shoulder.

"My bet is he already knows," she replied. "Someone does because they used it."

"Are you sure it wasn't Fido?" he asked. He could make a ruckus sometimes, after all. Fido looked around indignantly at the mention of his name in connection with such controversy. *I have not now, nor ever have been ...*

"I'm positive," she dismissed. "Besides, it would explain all the other weird noises and that window being left open."

"I just ..." he sighed, shaking his head. "You know what, let's finish pudding and look into it. I think I saw some torches in one of the storage cupboards."

# CHAPTER NINE

## Tomlinson Hall

## Part Two: Only Open Eyes Can See

Olivia had forgotten how dark the tunnel was but then, with a complete absence of light, is the darkness itself somehow less memorable? Robin, having never been in the tunnel before, had nothing to remember. Flashing their torches around, they took in the narrow corridor far more effectively than Olivia had managed with her iPhone. There were cobwebs everywhere yet, as Robin pointed out, there seemed to be a clear path through them.

"This would support the idea of someone using it regularly, and recently," he stated, pulling a face. Yes, but *who*, apart from Olivia that once? That was the question dancing before them, mercilessly shoving the fact that they didn't know in their faces.

With Robin and Fido there, Olivia lost her nervousness and became progressively more adventurous. Using an old umbrella she'd found, she cut through the remaining sea of cobwebs determinedly. The brick floors betrayed no footprints as they followed the tunnel. Olivia recognised the floor at the area where she'd turned back before. She checked the time, noting that she had no signal on her phone at the same time.

"*We're on our own down here,*" she mimicked in a 'damsel in distress' voice.

"*We're by ourselves but never alone*," he said, starting to laugh a deep evil laugh. This was stopped by a coughing fit brought on by the dust.

"Do you think …?" she began, an idea coming to her. "I think we're going downhill. Do you think this comes out somewhere in the village?"

"Maybe it did once, but it's probably blocked off now, health and safety and all that," he shrugged.

"And here we are, facing down fear, heading further in without our hardhats," she said, being the rearranged deep in deadpanned. They pressed on in silence for a moment, aside from Fido's panting.

A shadow loomed on the side of the tunnel. It appeared to be a knackered, dishevelled, distressed, threadbare, worn-out, ancient, or 'had seen better days' looking old cabinet. It didn't look exactly brand new either – one star review, could do better. Some may criticise the extended nature of the description, but they'd been in the tunnel a while and there was not a lot else to see, not to mention it broke up the terrible dialogue. As a result, let's dispense with any such enquiries as 'What's that?' or 'Is that a cabinet?' and get on with the story.

"You know, I think that's a cabinet," said Robin, lamely.

"Good heavens, what could it be doing in this tunnel?" Olivia responded, mordantly.

"I don't know, it's a conundrum," he rumbled, rocking his head from side to side as he spoke.

"I thought you said it was a cabinet," she said, touching her chin with her fingertips comically. Robin tried to open it but it was apparently locked. They examined it closely and Olivia blew the dust away to reveal an old sheet of paper. Carefully they unfolded it and tried to make sense of the faded spidery writing.

"Looks like a list," she murmured, pushing her glasses up her nose. "One hundred of this, one of that …"

"It's the *this and thats* which I can't make out," he muttered, squinting.

"No signal down here," she groaned, trying to get her translator app to work.

"You haven't got a magnifying glass app, have you?" he asked, raising an eyebrow.

"That's a great idea for an app!" she declared, writing it down in her draft emails. Carefully, Olivia pointed to the first word. "I think that's an 'I'."

"Inyat?" he tried, frowning.

"Impat?" she offered, leaning in closer.

"So, let us recap," he suggested, being silly. "One hundred impats." There was a lone 's' at the far end of the sheet but on the same line.

"Try lower down," she sighed. "Three hundred impats, one hundred 's', one hundred 'g', and one hundred 's' again ... why not two hundred?"

"More than one 's'?" he answered, vaguely.

"Okay, forget the inyat things, what's that word on the fourth line? *Saq* ... *Sapptire* ... *Sapphire*!" she yelled the last word, her voice echoing loudly. "Four hundred sapphires!" They stared at one another.

"Nah..." he said, shaking his head. "It can't be ..."

"Yes, it can, it can, look," she said, excited. "It's double 'p', which is correct for 'sapphire'."

"Are you sure?"

She sighed.

"Of course," she pouted, amused. "I might not be perfect in every way, but I am great at spelling things – even when I don't necessarily know what they mean." He gave a chuckle.

"All right, all right," he raised his hands in surrender. "I trust you."

"There's another sapphire down here, see – the word is the same, another four hundred – then – hey!" she jabbed at the figure of one thousand.

"Come on, that's an easy one, one thousand rubies," she said, amazed.

"Or roubles," he contended, without conviction.

"What's that one?" she asked. "One thousand seven hundred and twenty … or something …" She swore with frustration.

"I appreciate how crazy this sounds, but this is a list of treasures or something," he stated, looking up and down the tunnel. He'd suddenly become rather self-conscious.

"Baby," she whispered, eyes wide. "If we could find it …"

"Oh, come on," he groaned, already knowing where she was going. "This paper has probably been here hundreds of years, assuming it's real and presuming that we're understanding it correctly! The odds that any of it is still here …"

"We could save the Hall!" she pleaded. "It's worth a try, we can't do it ourselves and no one is helping us yet."

He let out a breath and stared down the tunnel again. It did go on – the tunnel, not the story.

"I just …" he said, worried she would feel let down. She sighed.

"I know it's a long shot … like a sniper league shot, but it's all we have," she continued.

"Yeah, but … fine," he growled, knowing she could be right. He just didn't like the idea of spending all night wandering around a tunnel in the hope of locating items on a list that might not even be there! She misunderstood his tone.

"We can still … you know … later," she said, smiling up at him. "I did promise never to use it against you." That earned her a smile.

"You did… alright, tomb raider, what do you want to do?"

She scanned the list again.

"There's a lot of stuff on this list … you'd need somewhere large to store it, right?" she reasoned.

"A bank safe comes to mind," he said, downcast. He hurriedly inserted some enthusiasm into his tone, though. Olivia always said he shouldn't be so negative. "But the next best thing would be a place like this!"

"Let's keep going," she said, slipping the paper into her pocket. She wrapped her arm around his as they walked and let out a tiny giggle. "This is so cool." He pulled a rictus smile.

They reached a split in the tunnel, one way going to the left and the other to the right.

"Left first, if we keep going left it will be easy to find our way out," he reminded her. These tunnels were not so wide as the original and they followed it along in silence.

It was after tiptoeing down a roughly cut set of steps that their path was blocked by a metal gate. They peered further along through the bars and tried to get it open, but it was locked.

"This proves there is something else down here! Right it is," sighed Olivia, gesturing. "We'll have to ask Peter if he's got any keys lying around."

"It proves someone decided to install a gate, and forgot to leave it unlocked," he muttered, starting to lose the will to live. "Good thing they didn't have fire escape regulations back then …"

"What are you going on about?" she hissed, amused.

"Nothing, my dear," he grinned, sweetly.

"Look, I bet you there's stuff down there, maybe not jewels, but old stuff!" she insisted. "A tenner?"

"Ten quid?" he asked. "All right, you're on." They were still in the passageway when they heard voices coming from ahead. They stopped instantly but Fido seemed undaunted. They listened hard but nothing was understandable at that distance. One thing was clear, though – it was a man and a woman. Carefully, they crept forwards until they reached another locked metal gate. A flicker of light flashed from another direction, and they worked out the next passage went from left to right rather than straight on.

"What was that?" asked Maisy, from some distance away.

"I didn't hear anything, probably just echoes," answered Edmund. Fido stuck his head through the bars, but Olivia managed to get a hold of his collar before he could escape. They waited anxiously, wondering if the game was up.

"Must have been, no one else could be down here and I've never seen any mice or rats," Maisy concluded. "Look, people will eventually figure it out."

"My wife has been dead a long time, I'm sure they'd forgive us," replied Edmund.

"I'm not talking about that," she stated. "They know you spoke to them before, and they might put two and two together."

"So did half the village when Olivia paid you a visit," he reminded her, unconcerned. "I imagine a few of them already suspect but no one can prove anything."

"At some stage it will come out," she insisted with a heavy sigh. "I thought you just liked to irritate them; I didn't realise you were serious."

"I'm only following the instructions I was given," he protested. "And no, while at first it was a bit of fun, I'm no longer enjoying it.

Thing is, even if we made it known, I'm not sure it would solve anything. It might make it worse."

"Andy and Tim would never let it rest, I grant you, but no one really cares what they think. Only their wealth prevents them from being social pariahs," she said.

"Do we have to do this down here? I've got some wine chilling in the fridge back at the church," he chuckled.

"We were talking about secrets, and this place seemed appropriate," she giggled. "Besides, I rather like it down here. Aside from the Hall itself, it's one of the few places in the whole village where no one can see you."

"That's true," he admitted.

Robin and Olivia strained their ears as the voices moved further away.

"What was that about?" was Olivia's pantomime whisper.

"So, there's a tunnel from, I'm guessing, the pub or wherever Maisy lives, to the church," he said, frowning deeply. "Interesting. We've not even explored the other way yet, either."

"I'm surprised they are an item but, like she said, if they're trying to keep their relationship a secret, where better to go than down here?"

"Why would they keep it a secret?" he asked, genuinely curious.

"Maybe she's married?" she offered, shrugging. "I got the impression she was single, but it's not like I directly asked her about it. She's the landlady, so …"

"Is this gate locked?" he asked, rattling it a little.

"That would be a yes," she said, eyeing the lock. It was a carbon copy of the other gate they'd found further back. It had the cobwebs to prove its age.

"Can we go back now?" he asked, an amused expression on his face.

"No choice," she groaned, disappointed. She was still harbouring fantasies about finding something interesting – apparently that was not going to happen.

*

Olivia opened her eyes sleepily and observed the sunlight streaming in through the windows. She reached out but couldn't find Robin. She sat up and perceived the empty room before putting her glasses on and strolling over to put on her dressing gown. She'd taken to wearing Anne's old one as it fitted her perfectly. She reached the library and saw Robin poring over several books with Fido yawning at his feet. She smiled and leaned against the door for a moment before going in.

"Morning, detective," she smiled. He looked up animatedly.

"I think Edward wrote that list we found," he explained excitedly. We're still not going to tell Peter or Kat about our discovery, are we?"

"Not a word yet," she nodded. "They'll be here soon. So, Edward hid some things down there from Jack?" He looked confused, then he realised she was talking about the wrong Edward.

"No, no, the original Edward Tomlinson, not the brother of the one who's left us this place," he clarified. She perched on his lap as she looked at the handwriting of the note and those in a few other samples he'd found. She couldn't deny it looked very similar.

"So, Edward wrote this list and left it down there?"

"Well, assuming it was him who left the list down there, yes," he replied. "I mean, assuming he didn't build that tunnel network, he would certainly have known about it."

"It also implies that we're the only people who've been in that tunnel section since the early 1800s, otherwise someone else would surely have found the list?" she questioned. "Yet we know someone's been using the tunnel to get in and out of the Hall without anyone knowing."

"We presume …" he began. Then his eyes went wide. "You don't think it's Jack?"

"As in, dead Jack?"

"You know another Jack?" he quipped.

"I don't think he's haunting the place …"

"No, maybe he's not dead at all and he's living somewhere down there in secret," he went on.

"Why?" she bluntly enquired. He paused and then let out a breath.

"Because he's got no money and he's pretending to be dead to escape paying off the debts!" he theorised. She looked at all the books on the table then into his eyes.

"How long have you been in here?" she giggled, kissing him. "I've told you before about obsessing over things, it's bad for you. You did get some sleep last night, right?"

"Only when you let me," he grinned, kissing her back.

"Anyway …" she said, wriggling free. "I thought of something else last night. Maybe Edmund has a key to the gate, and it was him who sneaked in here. After all, it was him who told us to dig around in here. Maybe he was trying to lead us to find the tunnels."

"That gate didn't look like it had moved in years," he sighed, standing up. "Come on, let's get some toast."

As they stood over the toaster, like hawks awaiting their prey to move, they speculated that there could be other secret passageways. The Hall had probably been around in Reformation times, so a priest hole was not out of the question – especially in a place with royal connections. St Nicholas's church had been rebuilt after Henry VIII and perhaps that passageway was an escape for the clergy when the chips were down.

"I can't imagine them running to the pub," he chuckled.

"Maybe it wasn't a pub back then," she responded. "We need to know more about the area's history."

"You're the expert; is there anything in the *Chronicles of Barnet* about priests?"

"Well, in the back there's a list of all the vicars from 1605, but the English Reformation was finished a couple of years before that," she mused, going over it as she spread the butter. "The previous church was destroyed, so … trouble is, all that was long before the Tomlinsons came here."

"So, you don't think there's a priest hole here?"

"Honestly, after that labyrinth we found last night, I would be surprised if there wasn't something like it around here," she said. "I've got no idea how to go about finding these things either, short of going around knocking on walls and things." He chuckled.

"Yeah, tricky to explain that to Peter and Kat."

"Yeah, explaining that our tactic is literally to go treasure hunting in response to the debts of the Hall wouldn't be the most productive of conversations," she acknowledged, sardonically.

"I think we should confront Edmund; he might have keys to the doors down there," he sighed. "I know he probably means us no harm, but the idea of him just wandering in whenever he likes doesn't exactly fill me with confidence."

\*

"They say everyone has one book in them and I think that's true. I also believe that everyone has one moment of absolute joy in their lives, a moment in time they will always remember and look back on," said Kat, sipping her tea. Olivia immediately tried to think of when that moment was for her. The first time Robin had kissed her? The first time she'd sped down a motorway when no other cars were there? That feeling of relieved contentment she got when she completed one of her projects? Then there was that lasagne she'd eaten in Milan when she'd been twelve …

"Tell me when that was for you?" Olivia asked, curious.

"September 1970," she answered, without hesitation. "A river of tequila, a mist of tobacco and the blare of rock music. It was so warm, and I felt like I was in heaven."

"Wow, you got a whole month there …" she said, not sure her own moments were up to that level.

"It was the best time of my life. I mean I've had other good times, of course, but that was the high point," she grinned. Olivia recognised the double meaning and shook her head as she smiled.

"It was the end of the sixties, we were all wild and full of hope, the revolution of love," she elaborated, with a defensive laugh.

"Yes … kind of lost their way though, didn't they?" she observed.

"Every generation does, sweetie. You start out so strong and gradually time takes its toll. I wouldn't change it for anything," she said. "Everyone has to have their time, but no one gets to keep it."

"Did you ever marry?" asked Olivia, as Robin and Peter walked past the doorway. Kat caught the flicker of Olivia's eyes.

"I wanted to but no, I didn't," she responded, sadly. "There was a man but we couldn't make it work."

"What happened?" asked Olivia, sympathy in her face.

"Families are complicated things, as you've no doubt discovered here," she said shrugging away the question. "Sometimes things just aren't meant to be." Sensing the other woman's discomfort, Olivia chose not to pry any further. Instead, she changed the subject.

"Yes, the Tomlinsons are a prime example. What happened to Thomas's sister, Mary? The book says she went to America but then there's no further mention of her. Is it possible she could have had children and the family still exists?"

"No, not that I've ever heard," replied Kat, thinking about it. "Tracey did some extensive research and no relatives could be found. She searched from 1830 through to the Civil War but there's nothing."

"So, she just died out there?" sighed Olivia sadly.

"No one really knows why she went to America, either. There was talk of a pregnancy that had to be hushed up, but it might have had more to do with her not getting along well with Thomas's wife. Did you read their correspondence?"

"Yes, couldn't make sense of all of it, but I got the impression that under all those enforced polite formalities they maybe hated each other," Olivia said. "It's just, I was thinking, if they did exist, living relatives, I mean, maybe they could help us."

"Yes, it's a nice idea but we're on our own here, I fear," Kat proclaimed as she placed her tea cup back in the saucer.

"Well, it might be a link to who the fourth beneficiary is and also why we've not seen them yet, if they're across the pond," she elaborated.

"If that is the case, it would also mean that whoever wrote the will would have to have known who they were and where they were. As you can see, the book says Mary was gone and no one else emerged," said Kat. "Jack, or whoever wrote the will, probably had no more information than what's in that."

"Yes, but no one knew where Jack went, either, he just vanished, a lot like Mary," persisted Olivia.

"All this is very possible, but how can we find anything out from here, and in the time we have?" asked Kat, seriously.

"I don't know," she conceded. "I just think I'm onto something here."

# CHAPTER TEN

# What about us?

The door closed and they were alone again. Olivia began to strap Fido's jacket on him with the spare batteries, the water, and the food. They were going down into the tunnels again and this time they were going to try the other direction. Robin sat at the table in the library, tapping the end of the pen ponderously on the papers before him. His gaze found the sword in the glass cabinet, and he remembered the dreams he'd had back in London. That all seemed so long ago now. He stood up and approached the glass to look more closely. Slowly he reached out a hand to open it.

"What in the name of silage, sanitation and sloppy seconds are you doing?" asked Olivia, who'd appeared in the doorway like a banshee. He recoiled and spun around guiltily with an involuntary yelp.

"Nothing!" he reflexively declared. She raised an eyebrow and noticed the sword.

"No! Absolutely not," she grinned, shaking her head. "You're like a big kid!"

"Says she who creeps around the place as if playing hide and seek. That's not a toy," he laughed.

"Well, I know, but what were you planning on doing with it? Opening letters? I don't see any enemies on the horizon, and I don't need rescuing!"

"I just wanted to hold it for a minute," he admitted, embarrassed. "I mean, that's a proper sword."

"I know … fine!" she groaned, rolling her eyes. "But be quick! Fido's ready and so am I."

"Makes a change," he mumbled.

"What was that, light of my life?" she asked, crossing her arms.

Carefully, Robin opened the cabinet and gently reached in to grab the sword. It was a bit heavier than it looked but he extracted it without incident.

"Whoa," he mouthed, turning it this way and that. "This is …" He unsheathed it and was amazed to see the blade was not only shiny but sharp as well. As he moved it, practising a few strokes from the movies, he heard a click coming from the hilt. He caught sight of her smiling and shaking her head.

"Want a go?" he beckoned, offering her the handle.

She made a pretence of looking uninterested before scuttling forward to take it. She held it up to the light and heard the tiny clicking sound. It had a red and gold tassel, like a lanyard, that dangled down from the grip.

"Careful," he cautioned, as she swished it around. She handed it back and they both heard the click.

"Let's hope it always made that noise. What is that?" she asked. They quickly determined it had something inside the grip and that the blade unscrewed. Much to their bewildered anticipation, Robin was able to open it, and a small silver key fell out. It was too small for the tunnel gates.

"What the actual …?" she trailed off.

"This place is full of surprises," he muttered, as spellbound as Olivia. He replaced the sword in its display cabinet as they looked around for anything that was locked. Nothing leapt out at them.

"Great – another mystery," she said with a little laugh. "Just what we needed." Robin took the key and examined it.

"This looks like it wouldn't be for a door at all, more like a case or a display cupboard," he mused, thoughtfully.

"It can wait. First, we must check out the other tunnel," she reminded him.

They headed downstairs. Fido looked up expectantly as they opened the wine cellar. He was anxious to move on fast – so, not an alcoholic. Torches on, they headed back into the secret tunnel. This time they turned left and quickly came to a narrow stairway cut into the rock that led down and to the right. The tunnel then made a series of turns as if it were circumventing something.

"No idea where we're going this time," Robin grunted. "Too many changes in direction."

"Weird," she muttered, also unsure. They knew that at least one of these passages went into the village, as evidenced by nearly bumping into the vicar and his mistress the previous evening. Yet they had no idea about the other gated off tunnel or this one.

"You know, I had a dream with that sword in," he reminded her.

"I'm still gutted you weren't dreaming about me," she deadpanned. "Still, on the positive side, I wasn't literally gutted by you when you were weaving it around either."

"I was just saying … maybe I subconsciously picked up on it because I knew it was hiding something, not because I wanted to hold it."

"Or, stop me if you've already thought of this, it's maybe because you've just not grown up yet," she said jokingly.

"Keep talking and I'll ban you from my fort," he chuckled.

They paused when they thought they heard something from ahead of them. Again, as Fido didn't seem remotely concerned, they went on, and soon they found the source. Running water. Apparently, they were crossing an underground stream.

"We must be under the woods, which means ... we're heading into the village again," Robin surmised.

"Yeah, but in a slightly different direction," she agreed. "Where else would he go? The police station?"

"Oh yeah, we've still got to go and check out that place," he grunted. "When you say *he* ...?"

"Well, Edward Tomlinson – it's got to be him. According to that book, he was a member of that crazy club in the early 1800s, and maybe they used to party down here or something."

"Maybe ... but they might be much older than that," he reminded her.

"Yes, but Edward burned all the records so we don't know who owned the Hall before the Tomlinsons," she said. He smiled.

"You're really into that book, aren't you?"

"Yes, it's fascinating and, given our situation, quite helpful. It doesn't mention these tunnels though so we're further in the tunnels than Tracey was," she replied.

"I can't understand how Peter and Kat do not know these are here," he reiterated, not for the first time. After all, it was impossible to reiterate something that hadn't been alluded to previously. "I mean, Edmund clearly knows, so – if they do know and haven't told us, then ... oh heavens! If he knows that they know that we know ..."

"Maybe they don't think it matters, if there is nothing down here – or they couldn't get through the gates either," she theorised.

"You've got a tenner riding on there being stuff here, remember? Or do you want to renege?" he chuckled.

"Can I borrow two fivers?" she jested.

"So much for that!" grunted Robin, seeing a dead end in the torchlight.

"Wait, is that a ladder?" asked Olivia as the torchlight bequeathed them with an alcove.

Sure enough, there was a hatchway in the ceiling of the tunnel, and an old metal ladder was concealed in the recess. Robin carefully climbed up and tried to open the hatch. It wouldn't budge and he thumped it a few times.

"Locked or blocked," he explained, needlessly. "I suppose it makes more sense than a dead end. Very long tunnel to lead to nowhere."

"Hello!" yelled Olivia, causing him to shush her.

"Don't! You might wake someone up," he warned.

"If this leads into someone's house and they don't know about it then they deserve to know," she complained.

"If they don't know what we know, how can we know if they deserve to know what we know?"

"Will you stop doing that? It was only just funny the first time."

The key he'd found in the sword was too small for the hatch and, it seemed to the layman and laywoman present, that the locks of the hatch were smaller than those of the barred gates in the tunnels. This felt like one of those video games where you had to find the keys to unlock something – oddly enough, they'd never been in that situation for real.

"Yes, I'm certain they would display great gratitude to us for telling them as we're getting arrested for trespassing!" he was quick to add.

"That's one way out of this situation," she muttered. "I think it's clear neither of us particularly wish to return to London. What about us? What if we can't save the Hall?" He paused and lowered his head for a moment.

"Repossession," he said, knowing he didn't have to. "Then I'd have to find another job …"

"You remember when we visited Beccles last summer? We were lying there talking, and we asked each other what we really wanted?" she asked, her voice softer.

"Course," he said, dropping fully back into the tunnel.

"You said that you wanted success and we agreed that it was opinion, chiefly our own opinions, that mattered most when deciding if we were successful or not. I said that, for some people, being able to live in London was a sort of success," she recalled.

"And I also said I wasn't sure about that," he hedged, not sure where she was going. "Wasn't it at that point you coined the phrase 'situation-ship'?"

"For years we've been taught that careers are the most important thing in our lives. Ever since we were about nine, anyway. I don't know if it's right," she concluded.

"You mean if teaching people that careers are the most important thing is right, or if it's okay for most other people but not us?" he clarified, uncertainly. She sighed.

"I don't know, being in this place – the Hall, I mean, not this tunnel specifically – over the last few weeks … it's been weird," she elaborated. "It's made me rethink things and look at them differently."

"Me too," he admitted, sombrely.

"Imagine if we end up saving this place … it could be ours forever."

"That's a big if," he replied, reminding her unnecessarily of the odds against them.

"I was thinking …"

"Oh boy," he grinned. She smiled and playfully punched him.

"So much of our lives have been big ifs, haven't they? Being born without illness, meeting and falling in love ... None of those things, if you think about them, are guarantees."

"Well, nothing is, if we really get down to it," was the evident philosophical response.

"So ... I think we're meant to be here, we're meant to live here," she replied with more certainty.

"I'm pretty sure some people want us to be here," he nodded, remembering the ghostly dreams he'd had back in London. "Though that might be less about us having it and more about preventing someone else from getting it."

They fell silent and Olivia shivered – the excitement could only keep the chill at bay so long. Before she could even look at him, Robin was already slipping his jacket around her shoulders. She smiled up at him almost shyly.

"If you're starting to think that the new success will be to secure the Hall, I admit I think you're right," he said. "I don't believe in anything supernatural or spiritual, as you know, but everything that has happened lately has made me think something or someone wants us here."

"We need to find the keys to those gates," she sighed determinedly.

"Search the Hall again?" he offered, levelly. It was fast becoming their hobby at this point.

"You take the upstairs and I'll take the downstairs," she suggested. He nodded.

Over the next few hours, while Fido sniffed around uselessly, Robin and Olivia did their best to go over the whole property on a non-forensic level. Just after three in the morning, they finally threw in the towel. After a long shower, they passed out and didn't wake up until they heard Fido scratching at the door and Peter tentatively calling to them from downstairs.

"Gosh!" groaned Olivia, after blearily glancing at her phone. "Robin!" Robin lurched awake and blinked at her in confusion. Fumbling with her dressing gown, she got the door open and was midway through calling out to Peter in response when she was flattened by Fido. Coughing and spluttering, she laughed as she pushed his wet nose away from her face. Robin stretched and stared down at them rolling around on the floor.

"Someone wants a walk!" he declared. Upon hearing one of his favourite words, Fido rushed at Robin instead.

Fido had many favourite words: food, steak, treat, park, food, fetch, Fido, fridge-magnet, and did someone mention food?

A few moments later, Olivia was munching on some toast that Peter had made for them while Robin and Fido braved the morning outside. She began re-reading the documents they had spent most of yesterday going over. Of course, nothing had changed, but if hope didn't spring eternal then it might spring them out of this while standing idle. Again and again, she asked herself who the fourth beneficiary was, where the keys they needed could be, and what was the link between them and Jack Tomlinson. She'd entertained the possibility that it was not Jack they were linked to but one of the others; however, which one? His duplicitous, gambling-mad brother Edward? What were the odds?

Olivia had obsessively combed through some of the historical books from the library, even going so far as trying to research the Ward family. The Wards had been close friends with Henry and Anne — perhaps more than just close? If it didn't cost so much money, Olivia would give serious consideration to doing a DNA check with Ancestry or some other firm. Lucre, however, was their problem, much as it had no doubt been Edward's and Jack's. She'd considered that if Jack knew about the tunnels, then it was likely there was nothing of worth down there, but if he hadn't known … but that didn't mean Edward hadn't already plundered them. The note from the cabinet gave her hope as it appeared not to have been touched and the writing seemed to be from the original Edward.

She knew he was an industrialist, possibly from Dublin in Ireland but, as the books all seemed to agree, no one knew for sure where he came from or how rich he was. Then there were the mysterious payments that had been doing the job of keeping the Hall afloat since the eighties. HRH ... Some modern incarnation of an old business set up by Edward back in the day? Her fingertips drummed out an irregular beat on the table as her agitation grew. They were getting nowhere! Going around and around in endless circles. Then an idea came to her ... they'd searched the tunnels, certainly the ones they had access to, and they'd gone over the Hall last night ... but they'd not yet searched the garden!

Pulling on Anne's old anorak, still with the last of her toast in her mouth, Olivia stumbled out of the door into the drizzle. Peter, midway through chopping up some firewood under the shelter of an old plastic side roof, glanced up as Olivia walked across the lawn towards the small maze of hedges around the fountain. He stood there watching, axe in hand, as the rain began to intensify. Entering the maze, Olivia went from one ancient statue to the next to examine them more closely.

\*

"Morning!" hailed Kat when she met Robin and Fido on their walk.

"Morning!" called Robin in response.

"Hello, Fido," Kat smiled, stroking him, despite how wet he was.

"You just coming to the Hall?" he guessed without difficulty.

"I was, yes," she smiled, squinting up in the rain. "Not a day for it, but we have more pressing things to think about than the weather." They continued on, a little slower now so that Kat could keep up. She yawned suddenly and in a way that he suspected she wanted him to remark on.

"Late night was it, Kat?" he asked, not all that interested.

"Indeed, I fear my cottage may have ghosts, Robin," she chortled. "There I was, sleeping soundly after a day of thinking, when I was awoken by some peculiar thumping noises."

"Probably your imagination, I'm sure," he smiled, reassuringly. "Happens to me all the time."

"The thumping could indeed have been just my old mind playing tricks, or even an animal, but the voice is a little harder for me to dismiss," she went on.

"Voice?" he asked as anyone would.

"Yes, I could have sworn I heard someone calling out but from somewhere beneath me," she replied, evidently perplexed.

"What did they say?" he asked, not really taking it seriously.

"Sounded like hello but, I'll be honest, my hearing is not what it used to be," she chuckled. "Too many tequilas back in the day, I expect." They reached the driveway and began to meander down it towards the Hall.

"I fear neither of us are young enough to justify monsters under our beds," he jested pleasantly.

"I should hope so!" she agreed. "It does make you think, though, doesn't it? I mean, suppose there really was someone there with me – if not a ghost, then a person, or even more than one person?"

"Highly unlikely," he said, easy going. That was when the penny dropped. "Sorry, when did you say this happened?"

"Just past midnight, not quite one," she said after a moment of consideration.

He worked it out quickly – that was when they'd found the hatch in the roof of the tunnel last night! Olivia had called out and he was sure she'd said hello. Had that tunnel been directly under Kat's cottage?

"Weird," he settled on, not sure what else to say.

"Probably just hearing things, as you say, didn't half give me a fright though," she responded.

"I can imagine …" he began, but was interrupted.

*

With a squeal, Olivia discovered the water was just as cold as she'd feared. Having searched every statue, she had, by this stage, convinced herself that the only other place anything could be hidden, short of under the earth somewhere, was in the fountain. After hesitating briefly when standing on the stone wall surrounding the water, she stepped forward and plunged into the lily pads. Ducks quacked and flapped away in surprise, even Eric the local goose looked on, dumbfounded. Breathing hard, she gritted her teeth and waded over to the central feature. It was an intricately carved statue of Venus.

"Okay, sorry, but it's time for your cavity search," snarled Olivia, the cold making her shiver.

There were gaps and tiny ledges to explore, and Olivia was halfway through doing so when something splashed loudly next to her and she shrieked. Fido was barking loudly and Kat was only just managing to hold him back.

"What are you doing?" cried Robin, lunging towards her.

"I was … what do you think I'm doing?"

"Looks like you're feeling up the stone goddess here, but I'm guessing you have another explanation?" he replied, nearly overbalancing.

"I'm just searching it," she replied under her breath.

"Okay, you're crazy, we've been in this place too long, and here I am trying to blame all our problems on the internet," he said. She laughed. That was when she found something. Her hand was under the water level but there was a crevice there. She yanked it free and nearly lost it but somehow managed to shove it into her pocket.

"Help me out with dignity, please," she requested. He raised an eyebrow and for a second, she thought he was going to dunk her, but luckily he chose to be merciful.

"Are you all right?" asked Kat, looking worried.

"Yup," smiled Robin, hauling Olivia out of the water. They stood there dripping and panting.

"What happened?"

"I fell," stated Olivia, sheepishly. "And even though I didn't need rescuing, thanks."

"Nothing worse than a soaked feminist," he chuckled, putting his arm around her.

Later, as steam rose over the top of the shower door, Robin sighed as he took a seat on the lavatory.

"So what did you find?" he asked patiently.

"Who says I found anything?" she grinned as she rolled her shoulders under the hot water.

"Your smug face," he replied, knowingly.

"Catch!" she called, in warning. The small wooden box landed in his hands accurately. He heard the rattle as he shook it.

"Key," he surmised, trying to open it.

"You can thank me later," she sighed. "Truth is, it was a long shot. I figured the only place we've not searched was the garden, so …"

"Nice," he said, trying to force it open. "You're going to love this, but I think it's locked."

"Well, of course it is! What would be the point of hiding something in a little box like that for years and leaving it open to the elements?" she pointed out. "Will the key we found in the sword open it?" Robin tried, and it did indeed open it. Another key was inside; however, he instantly knew it would not fit the gates underground as it was far too small. He explained his findings as he stripped off.

"So, we still need to find something else that's locked," she groaned. She jumped suddenly when he joined her in the shower.

"You remember that cabinet, the old wooden one down in the tunnel?" he asked.

"The one we found the note on? Yes, of course, it was the only furniture down there," she recalled.

"Did we actually open the drawers on it?"

"Um …"

# CHAPTER ELEVEN

## Whispers from the Dead

"Never seen this place so quiet, yet so full," confided Toggle as she looked around the Old New Inn. Jake eyed her over the rim of his pint glass, having been in mid-sentence about a new tent he was planning to buy. This one was something special, a four-season tent with inner mesh and incredible ventilation so that it could deal with both the harsh winter and the heat of the summer. According to the measurements, it would be more than large enough for Toggle and himself to camp in.

"… seams with no sign of a loose thread," he concluded with a sigh. He loved Toggle, he really did, but she seemed to have no interest in woodcraft and tents. All she wanted to do was read, eat, and take photos of nature. It was quite tragic really, she had the hardiness of a born outdoors-woman, he just couldn't understand it.

He looked around with a slight frown as he removed his tweed jacket and let it hang from the back of his chair. She was right, the pub did seem to be full, but everyone was either staring in silent thought or engaging in conspicuously hushed conversations.

"You could ask Maisy what's going down?" he suggested tactfully.

"Why don't you ask her?" she grinned, knowing full well why.

"I can't make eye contact with her, not after what happened before," he retorted, pleadingly. "Come on! Please!"

"Okay," was her mordant, long-suffering response. He stroked his beard as he watched her go, not even bothering to hide that he was curious too. Not much happened in Albany-on-Lea, which was why the surrounding land made for great camping opportunities.

Toggle arrived at the bar and smiled over at Maisy. Maisy disengaged with Agatha and came over. Her hand was already reaching for a fresh glass, a reflex she'd developed many years ago.

"Same again, love?" she asked, her tone somewhere between feigned interest and terminal ennui.

"Thanks. What's going on?" Toggle asked, leaning in closer. Maisy gave a cheeky grin in response.

"You're not the newest people in the village anymore and the newcomers have, shall we say, inadvertently stirred the pot," she paraphrased.

"Tell me more."

"You know Tomlinson Hall?"

"Yes, we camped in the woods near it a few times … last November, I think," she replied, nodding. "A beautiful building, I've often wondered what it must be like inside."

"Very soon, it will be under new ownership," Maisy said, turning away to pour the drinks. Toggle produced her card and waited as the pints were pulled expertly.

"So … I thought Jack Tomlinson didn't have any children," she whispered, wide-eyed. "I don't think he could, could he?" Maisy shrugged deadpan, as they waited for the payment to be approved.

"So, when you said new, you meant really new, like us?" she surmised. "Are they distant relatives?"

"My informant says the connection is tenuous, but the will has been read and we must all follow its instructions for as long as it's possible to do so," was the long-winded answer.

"Your informant?" chortled Toggle, enjoying the intrigue. "You're not going to self-destruct in ten seconds, are you?"

"Depends how drunk I get," winked back Maisy. Toggle laughed.

"So, who are they?"

"Robin Meadows and Olivia Higgins from London," she replied, leaning on the bar. "Oh, and Fido."

"Who's Fido?"

"Their dog," spelt out Maisy as if it were obvious.

"They have a dog!" smiled Toggle, who loved dogs.

"They do."

"So … they now own Tomlinson Hall?"

"Well, not exactly. Polly-Ann Smyth, them, and an anonymous individual do," she replied. She then gave details about the will reading and the mystery of the fourth beneficiary.

"And she fainted right there in the church?" asked Toggle, eyes wide.

"Probably in shock. I mean Jack has been gone a long time, but I've been told what went on before," she answered. "Besides, nobody had ever showed up. They buried the empty coffin last week."

"My God, and to think we were lying in a field staring up at the clouds, convinced we weren't missing anything," giggled Toggle.

"Oh, don't you believe it. Nothing much happens here but when it does, hold onto your seats!"

"Yeah," nodded Toggle. "So … who do you think the fourth is?"

"Some think it's Peter," Maisy responded, artfully. "Others refuse to speculate openly."

"And what do *you* think?" grinned Toggle, seeing through the evasion. "I thought nothing happened in this village without you knowing."

"Normally that's true, but even I have my off days," she shrugged. "I think that whoever it is, it's likely to be another stranger. Everyone knows Jack wouldn't want his Hall to end up with Andy King or Tim Williams. Though I'm told however that it may end up falling into their hands anyway."

"How so?"

"Robin and Olivia aren't wealthy enough and neither is Polly-Ann," she elaborated. "In a few weeks, unless a miracle happens, they'll have to hand it over to the relevant authorities."

"Oh no, that's dreadful," Toggle replied. "How much do they need?"

"Millions, I would imagine," shrugged Maisy. "Don't forget all this is second-hand information and could be subject to exaggeration, inaccuracy, falsehood and misunderstanding."

"Got it," she said, picking up their drinks and scampering back to Jake. "Guess what?" she enthused as she retook her seat. Jake grunted in response as he continued to frantically read reviews about the tent.

Quietly, Toggle reiterated everything Maisy had told her.

"So, what do you think?" she asked, earnestly. Jake looked up and momentarily his eyes glazed over before he answered.

"It's the weight that concerns me," he said, deep in thought.

"The wait? Wait for what?" she asked excitedly. "Like, how long it will take before they have to give up?"

"I mean, room isn't a problem, it's more a question of how far, if you see what I mean?"

"What?"

"This new tent," he replied, as if confused. She nodded slowly.

"Right … yeah."

\*

"Asking Edmund for help is the only logical thing to do, he's obligated to do so, or at least he can advise on who can assist us," said Peter. "There is some question as to the conflict of interest he will have. While, to my knowledge, he's never expressed an interest in owning the Hall, the survival of the village itself will be on his mind. He knows how integral this place is to it, and wouldn't wish to see it fall into the hands of the Kings."

"Can't we get the whole village to own it? Their combined wealth could do it, even though it would come down to percentage ownership?" suggested Robin. "That way, while some would own more than others, no one would be able to change anything easily."

"They'd never agree, and the two richest will stop at nothing to own this utterly – that's why they've not approached us yet," said Kat. "They will wait until the last moment – when they perceive us to be most desperate."

"We cannot support this place without help," Robin reminded her with a sigh. "Peter, when you called the bank, what did they say again?"

"They said they were not allowed to say who was putting money into the account, so we still don't know who HRH is," he answered.

"More coffee?" yawned Olivia, getting up from the chair.

"You sure we can afford it?" he remarked, with a raised eyebrow. "Perhaps this fourth beneficiary is just an invention of Jack's, to keep everyone guessing."

"To try to confuse or pacify the Kings for a while," murmured Kat, deep in thought. "Could be – only the solicitors would know."

"And that's another thing – who's paying them? They don't do this kind of thing for free," ranted Robin, starting to get frustrated.

"I believe the fourth beneficiary is real, but won't reveal

themselves until the time is right," said Olivia from the kitchen. "You know? When we're all about to give up. I'm not going to say it's the only explanation as it's not, but we're trapped between too many unknowns."

"By design, most likely," remarked Peter, sadly.

"Yes, but *whose* design?" persisted Robin, unable to let it drop.

"It's no good, I'm going to have to have a nap," stated Olivia, heading back into the hallway. "Wake me if you have a breakthrough."

"Didn't you sleep well, love?" asked Kat, curious. She didn't guess that Robin and Olivia had been up most of the night, searching the whole place.

"No, it's the way it goes, lot on my mind lately," she smiled in response. She knew she needed to keep her strength up for that evening's activities.

Robin too was showing signs of exhaustion and kept finding missed calls from Arni on his phone. Some time ago he'd put it on silent – probably unwise, given the circumstances, but he'd needed time to think. He was surprised how long ago it seemed that he'd last spoken to him.

London seemed like a mythical place, lost to time: now he was living and breathing Tomlinson Hall. It probably looked, at least from the perspectives of Kat and Peter, that Robin and Olivia only slept on the problem. They couldn't come up with anything themselves, either, but he felt the keen pressure to save the situation.

Notes from *Chronicles of Barnet – Legacy of the Tomlinsons* by Professor of History Tracey Stannett MSc (1961 – 2014):

*Of course, as is well known, matters came to a head in 1985. Edward Tomlinson finally died of liver cancer and Jack inherited the hall. Too late for anyone to save it, some would argue. It should be noted that due to missing Henry's funeral back in 1973, Jack saw to it that Edward wasn't buried in the family plot. It was rumoured that Anne too approved of this decision and records at the church corroborate this sentiment. Now, it has to be said that Jack already knew that what he was inheriting was no blessing. Edward had burned his way through the family fortune and ruined the businesses set up by the family in the past. Jack couldn't afford to keep the Hall, nor could he keep the debt collectors at bay.*

*It was at this point that some items of great sentimental value were sold in order to pay off some of the debt. These items included a diamond necklace given to Gwendoline Tomlinson by Queen Victoria back in 1880, several first editions of Shakespeare, a sizeable Roman coin collection (this possibly contained an Aureo medallion of Massenzio, but the private collector refused to confirm that), some Chinese vases, and numerous other artefacts. Jack was forced to sell these things to try to save the Hall, and he almost succeeded in stabilising the debt. Things were so grim that, when Anne died, he struggled to deal with the financial side of things concerning her funeral.*

*Indeed, according to all who were there at the time, and those who agreed to talk about it, it was the day after his mother's wake that Jack left the village, never to return. He set things up so the debt increase would be slow, and the Hall would be looked after. Once again, we enter the realm of speculation. It's unknown if Jack ever intended to return, but all who knew him expressed doubt that he'd stay away indefinitely. It is also believed that he went abroad to pursue a way of saving the Hall. The Hall itself had been left unoccupied once before, between the years of 1901 and 1921, but at the time of writing this, April 2012, I can say this is the longest period of dormancy so far (that we know of).*

*The last semi-credible sighting of Jack Tomlinson was in 2010 in Paris, when an old army friend thought he saw him in the crowd near the Wall of Love. It's true that some tourists once came to Tomlinson Hall in the summer of 1992 and apparently encountered Jack himself, even though the significance of his identity was only revealed to them later. The reason this encounter requires a larger than usual 'allegedly' with it, is because the man these people described didn't particularly resemble Jack. Again, some financial activities took place in 1997 that could only have been Jack himself, but he could not be found at the time.*

It was getting dark again. Peter and Kat had made themselves scarce, but the Hall itself seemed almost indifferent to Robin and Olivia. It was as if it had put its guard down and no longer regarded them as intruders. Olivia, after managing to sleep for a few hours, was scrabbling around in the library, trying to find any useful information, literally flicking through pages of books that in no way could help in the hope of stumbling across written notes. She'd had some joy in finding notes from various Tomlinsons, but nothing useful yet. Mainly, they were makeshift comments on the backs of newspapers, and even a shopping list. So deep in concentration was she that she failed to notice the rain hammering against the windows.

A flash of lightning finally caught her attention but, unlike in the car, she felt much safer in the Hall and simply ignored the meteorological bombardment. The thunder rolled loudly as Robin entered the room. He stared out at the rain for a long moment.

"Ready?" he asked, a torch in each hand.

"Yes, haven't had any luck here," she sighed, pushing her glasses up her nose. "Hey, I was wondering … what tools are kept around here? If we can't open the gate, then maybe you could force it open?"

That idea had occurred to him, but although the gates were old, they weren't corroded, and so he wasn't sure he could manage it.

"It would make a lot of noise," he pointed out.

"Who's going to hear us with that going on out there?" she shrugged.

"We don't know, that's the issue. I mean, we know that at least two other people know that the tunnels exist, even if they might not have access to all of them. I'd rather not advertise the fact that we know too." Olivia made a noise of reluctant agreement.

"I was wondering what other options we had should we be unable to find the key," she elaborated.

"We'll talk to it sternly," he smiled.

Entering the tunnels was becoming shockingly mundane by this point. The darkness was more an inconvenience than a source of intrigue and unease. The storm was reduced to nothing more than a muffled, distant rumble. The underground stream that crossed the tunnel would soon be gushing after all the rainfall. Would it flood? The notion of being trapped down there in freezing water was not one that encouraged jocundity.

It was hard not to think about what else might have gone on underground all those years ago. Wild parties? After all, according to the book, Edward Tomlinson had been a member of the Hellfire Club. Who knew what sort of debauchery he got up to in his day. Robin couldn't help but wonder if Rupert had been into smuggling and theft. Alright, if any of his booty was still down there somewhere, they'd probably have to give it back to wherever it had come from, but there could be a reward … Now he knew he was clutching at straws, not those awful plastic ones but the new paper, environmentally friendly variety.

They swiftly found the cabinet again. It wasn't like it could grow legs and walk off in a fit of pique. Robin sized it up in his mind, wondering how easy it would be to force it open should the key not work. It looked sturdy, if a little old, and he'd rather not have to damage what was probably an antique on the off-chance there was something useful inside. Much to their relieved delight, the key did fit, and they unlocked the cabinet. Inside was a large metal key, just sitting there, plain as anything, in the dust on the shelf, residing alongside a large supply of smug patience.

*Were you looking for me all this time? Fancy that! Next, you'll be expecting me to open some doors for you.*

"Locks and keys," chuckled Robin, in triumph.

"Looks like it should work," she said, considering the locks that the gate had. They traversed the next passageway somewhere between a quick walk and a jog, and reached the gate that led into the area where they'd overheard Edmund and Maisy. Carefully, they inserted the key and opened the gate. It gave a little high-pitched screech as it moved, and they stared at one another for a moment. Bit of WD40 needed on that … They entered and pulled the gate shut again, but didn't lock it. Excited, they began to pad along again in the torchlight. Now they were in uncharted territory once more, the caution returned.

The distant sound of music and talking reached them as they approached the end of the tunnel. There was a door at the end and light was coming from under it, seeping through into the darkness like the warm glow of candlelight. Robin slowly opened it, letting in the light from inside the pub. Mick looked up just in time to see a bookcase swing away and made eye contact with Robin. He froze, beer just short of his lips. Robin gave a smile and Olivia gave a little wave as they closed the door quickly. Mick blinked a couple of times, eyed the beer, shrugged, and continued drinking.

"So, this way leads to the pub … let's try the other way," Robin whispered.

"Handy little shortcut if it's raining like tonight," she jested.

Passing by the gate they'd unlocked earlier, they then followed the tunnel in the opposite direction. It wasn't very far at all. The door at the end didn't open; there seemed to be something blocking it but, after listening carefully, they thought they could hear organ music.

"It's the church," stated Robin with conviction. "Makes sense, what with the landlady and the vicar meeting down here. The church is right across the green from the pub."

"Let's get back and lock the gate again; we don't want anyone else figuring out how to get into the Hall," she replied.

"Maybe they didn't tell us about these tunnels because they were worried we would deny them access or something," pondered Robin. "To be honest, if those two want a bit of private time, I've no objection to them using this place."

"It must be tough to find some isolation in a village of this size," she concurred. "So, we can rule those two out? You know, from our list of suspects of who was sneaking around during the night?"

"I thought that was you and Fido," he grinned.

They returned to the first gate and locked it once more. They did discuss the possibility that there may be more than one key for it. Trouble was, there was no easy way to figure that out. Retracing their steps in the dark without any tracing paper at all wasn't easy, but somehow they managed it. It was probably due to their many years' experience as forest ranger story readers that saved them. The second gate looked just as imposing as the first, most likely annoyed that its only real purpose in the world was to swing back and forth and, lately, it hadn't even been allowed to do that.

Indeed, so long had it been since it had moved that they had a lot of trouble trying to open it. First, the key wouldn't fit, then it would but it wouldn't turn, then it thought about turning but was discouraged due to its lack of success in life. We've all been there. At last, after many seconds of persistence, the lock finally clicked, and the gate opened. The last gate had squeaked a little, but this thing set their teeth on edge with a horribly sped-up rendition of Country Gardens.

*

As the storm raged, and people realised they weren't going to be able to leave the pub at their usual times, animosity flared. Most of them just didn't get on; in fact, they were point-blank incompatible. Maisy watched as Andy and Tim sought to wind each other up in contests of one-upmanship, while Agatha and Enid did their best to de-escalate things. Sam was no help at all, laughing at the two other men at regular intervals and earning glowers from both. Only Toggle and Jake had escaped; having the very latest in survival ponchos, they'd fled to the safety of their tent earlier.

Maisy approached Mick who was sitting at the bar, his back to everyone else.

"You all right? You've been quiet tonight," she said.

"Ah, I was just listening in," he replied, smugly. "Who do you think will get the Hall in the end?"

"I know who I want to get it, and it's no one on that table," she muttered. "I've not met Robin yet, but I've met Olivia and she's very nice. I don't know much about them, but they would be an injection of much needed youth in this place. Jake and Toggle are a bit aloof to be community types."

"Much like myself," he smiled. He liked Jake, and the two of them often spoke about gear and machines together. Such discussions would bore anyone else to death, but Mick spent long periods of time without talking to anyone so really enjoyed them when they happened.

"This village will disappear within the next twenty-five years if something doesn't happen," she stated with certainty. "I know young people bring problems, but they also bring life. I never saw this place when it was vibrant, did you?"

"I remember when I was a child, it was reasonably active. Trouble is, you're from London. It's always active there so I can't really say," he replied, with a sigh. "I remember going to the school before it closed for the final time. It was a nice place in its way. Nothing lasts forever, though?"

"True, don't I know it," she sighed, entering a reverie of her own.

"Thing is, if it weren't for London and other cities, villages like this would be more active and no one would move away," he pointed out. "I'm not sure when this idea of owning your own house and moving away from your family started, but you can see the consequences. However, imagine having to spend the rest of your life with the Kings." That made her laugh.

"Rain's really coming down now," she said, looking at the windows. "Washing away all the dust."

"Symbolic?"

"Yes, I'd love a drink, thanks."

# CHAPTER TWELVE

## The Past, the Treasures and the Reckoning

The passageway didn't go on for long. After a short, irregular ramp and a turn to the right, Robin and Olivia entered a large room. It was empty, save for two holes. One was a stairway leading down and the other was much wider and had chains leading down from some mechanism above them. It had gears and wheels and looked very much like something out of the industrial revolution which, they supposed, it had to be.

"Platform lift," hissed Robin, in comprehension. Olivia nodded and then pointed to a narrow set of steps leading downwards.

Together, breathless, they darted down the stairs and came to a halt in a much larger room. They were silent as they scanned with the torches. Rows of wooden shelves took up most of the room, each one crammed with crates, some exposed, while others had covers draped over them. It was like something out of *Indiana Jones*.

Olivia's eyes widened and she smiled as she gripped Robin's hand so hard he yelped. She knew there was a big chance that all these boxes would be empty, or full of rubbish; however …

"I knew it!" she whispered, still looking around.

"I owe you a tenner," he breathed, also enthralled. She tentatively took a step forward and they slowly approached the first set of shelves. They knocked on the crate, which didn't budge. Crouching to examine the one nearest the floor, it was evident it had been there for some time, judging by the cobwebs and dust.

"On three?" he asked, gripping it. She took the other side.

"Watch your feet, babe," he cautioned, making sure he was clear. "Two, six, three."

With their combined strength, they were able to slide the first crate from the shelf onto the ground. It landed with a loud crash, and a vaguely metallic noise. Olivia held the torches and waited as Robin wrestled the lid off, coughing in the dust wave. As it slid away, golden ingots shone as the light found them. A silence fell as they both just stared.

"No …!" she mouthed at last. Robin reached in and picked one up. It had no markings – none that he could see, anyway, as he turned it this way and that. Olivia too handled one and marvelled at it. Neither of them had ever seen that much gold before, never mind handled it.

"Ingots!" she hissed, now understanding what they couldn't read before. Robin slowly rose to his full height, smacked his head on the shelf above, and cried out before trying to get an idea of the scale of this find. Olivia continued to rummage in amongst the ingots, after distractedly asking after his health. Robin saw the true scale of their find when he climbed on to the sets of shelves and saw many other small boxes sitting on top of the larger ones.

"Well …" he managed. Still holding his own (ingot), Olivia reached his side and looked at what he was checking out.

"There's loads of them," she whispered, suddenly unable to speak properly. "Even with Peter's help it will take days to get this lot out …" She was quaking with excitement, her torch shaking in her hand. Robin was finally able to break free of his own stunned silence.

"No, we only need the one ingot to show them. Then we'll have to declare the find and get it all certified and everything … then …"

"Then, if we get to keep it, we can use it to settle the debt!" she squeaked, almost crying.

"Look, don't get your hopes up – this might still not end well for us," he said, trying not to get carried away. "Imagine if it was stolen or something!"

"There could be a reward! Okay, so … do you want … tomorrow, when Peter and Kat get here … do you want to just put one of these on the table in front of them, all smug, and say nothing until they mention it?" she giggled, trying not to collapse into hysterics. He laughed.

"That's … do you think we could get one of the crates up?" she questioned, curious.

"We can try it once your dad tells us what we need to do about it," he concurred.

"I'll ring him as soon as we get out," she promised, already fumbling with her phone.

"Babe, it's a little late …"

"Nonsense! He won't mind. Knowing him, he'll probably want to drive down here right away," she dismissed.

"Let's hope he has more luck than we did trying to find this place," he mused, rolling his eyes.

It would turn out that Olivia was quite right to call her father immediately. Apparently, and neither of them knew this (most other people wouldn't have either, on account of never finding any treasure), you could be fined, or imprisoned for up to three months for failing to report a find. Basically, they had to report it to the local coroner within fourteen days! The Portable Antiquities Scheme was the mechanism with which to do this. Long story short, as with practically anything that involved legalities, there was a form to fill in. This proved very difficult as they couldn't really quantify what they had found. Also, the fact that they were joint temporary owners of the property was a complication.

After three mugs of coffee and a chat with a very understanding clerk in the coroner's office, a site visit was arranged for the next day so it could be audited, and, well, hopefully they'd be allowed to keep it. There was no point in trying to sleep and they gave up on the idea of their little joke with the ingot. Robin pointed out they might have to consider explaining to Peter and Kat precisely why they'd not confided in them. Due to the size of the find, the coroner and his team couldn't get there soon enough and promised to arrive by eight in the morning (assuming they didn't get lost).

Robin took Fido for his walk early as he was too anxious to just wait (Robin, not Fido). Olivia waited in case anyone needed to call them, and treated herself to a hot chocolate – her first of the year!

It was that time of day when dawn began, a more optimistic kind of twilight, about six in the morning. Fido tugged furiously on the lead, eager to get going as always, despite being up all night as well. Exhaustion was starting to catch up with Robin by this point, and he just let Fido pull him along in a daze. He didn't notice Kat until he nearly collided with her.

"Morning," she said with a smile.

"Hi," he groaned, clearing his throat. "Sorry, bit tired."

"I wanted to say something to you," she said, somehow keeping pace. Fido blanked her completely, but she didn't seem to mind.

"No worries," he smiled, blearily. Inwardly, he was hoping that he would be able to stay awake for the audit.

"Are you going to marry Olivia? I think you should," she said bluntly. This made him halt in his tracks, completely taken by surprise.

"What?" he blurted. The old woman smiled up at him, almost pleadingly.

"Not everyone gets the chance," she said with a significance he wasn't sure he understood. "It's clear she loves you and while there's never an ideal time to marry or to have children, this time might be the best for you." He just stared down at her, agape. He had to have passed out on the road somewhere and this was some sort of dream. What was she doing wandering the forest paths, anyway? He managed an awkward laugh.

"I … I do love her, obviously," he choked out.

"You will be happy together," she assured him, very seriously.

The truth was he had once before thought about marriage, but their generation didn't really do marriage. It was expensive, unfashionable, and often ended in divorce. He was pretty sure Olivia would say yes if he asked, but they'd never talked about it.

"This is …" he laughed awkwardly. "I …"

"You will need this," she said, handing him a presentation box. The red velvet of the ring box felt smooth but worn as if it was much older than it looked. Again, what little wind he had left escaped his sails and rendered him becalmed.

"I can't take this …" he blethered, not sure what was going on.

"That's quite correct, which is why I'm bestowing it on you," she responded flatly.

He opened the box in silence to behold a golden ring. It was grand, he had to admit. Some sort of diamond was the centre stone, and it was supported by two side stones which, to his untrained eye, could be rubies. When he looked up again, Kat was some way down the path he'd originally come down.

"Wait!" he began, still a bit shocked. She stopped and turned to face him but didn't say anything. Deciding that he needed to get back and that he would talk to her later about it, he just thanked her. "I'll see you later," he called. Kat waved before walking away.

There wasn't much further to go before he arrived back at the Hall, but his mind was running in circles now. What on earth was all that about? Was she ill or something? Should he marry Olivia? What if she said no? He hid the ring in his coat pocket and tried to remember what else they had to do that day. There was the audit first; until the outcome of that, everything else was still very much up in the air. He remembered that tiredness could kill and figured he'd better try to grab some sleep before they arrived.

Peter was there when he got back.

"Olivia's told me everything!" he said, thrilled. "I always knew that there had to be secret passageways somewhere here, but I could never find them."

"I'm sorry we didn't let you know about them sooner," he replied, awkwardly.

"Not at all, it's your Hall," he chortled as if it was nothing. "I would like to go down with you later when the examiners arrive, if that's okay."

"No problem. We're going to have to talk about a certain other passageway," he said, remembering. He trusted Peter completely at this point, so he wasn't worried that he would make trouble for Edmund and Maisy, but nonetheless they would have to talk about it.

Shortly after eight, the coroner and his team arrived. One of the young interns asked whether she could film some of the finds for her YouTube channel and, so long as she never gave away the location, everyone was fine with it. Robin and Olivia felt a bizarre stab of pride at discovering all this. The size of the find had even the coroner in awe. He explained that there were no hallmarks or symbols on any of it, so a lot of it was completely unidentifiable. After a few hours of examination, where his team documented as many as they could, they took the rest away for a more detailed study.

Given the odd situation, the mid-will beneficiaries, ownership of the Hall, and the debt itself, the coroner promised to prioritise the analysis and let them know as soon as he knew. By the time they left it was early afternoon, and Robin and Olivia had been able to catch a few hours of sleep while they were moving the treasure around.

"I can't believe moonlighting ever caught on," yawned Robin.

"You know what I read earlier today?" she asked.

"No?"

"Neither do I. I can't remember because of sleep deprivation," she complained.

"At least you didn't get hallucinations, like me," he chuckled.

"Not yet," she laughed sleepily. Robin sighed dramatically before turning over to bury his face in the pillow.

"It will be lunch time soon," he said, his voice muffled. That was when he remembered his bizarre conversation with Kat earlier that morning.

"I'm surprised we've not seen Kat yet today," he remarked, subtly.

"You can't see anything because a pillow is covering your eyes," she drawled, unbothered. She sat up and stretched before yawning. After half-heartedly adjusting her hair, she prodded him a few times.

"Come on, or Peter will come up to get us. We can ask if he's seen her. Maybe she showed up but cleared off when she couldn't see us?" Yawning and lethargic, they shuffled down the stairway together. Peter emerged from a doorway which led into the hall and beamed up at them.

"Ah, good evening, sleep well?" he asked, without a hint of sarcasm.

"No," grunted Robin, too tired to pretend.

"Jolly good," he replied, not really listening. "Tea's on the go." They sat in the north living room and watched as Fido sluggishly gnawed on a bone.

"So," breezed Peter, crossing his arms. "How much do you think it's worth?"

"No idea. I'm still not sure if we've found everything down there," admitted Robin.

"I got up to two hundred quid and it's definitely more than that," deadpanned Olivia, helpfully. "Have you seen Kat today?"

"I have not," he replied, frowning. "I did call her cottage earlier, but got no answer."

"After lunch, we should call in on her, just to be sure everything's all right," suggested Peter, smiling. "Who knows? Perhaps she too has made a discovery."

\*

Edmund panted as he staggered into the bar. He was not used to rushing around anymore but, after the conversation he'd just had, he couldn't resist hurrying.

"Everyone listen, I have absolutely incredible news that halts everything!" he declared, poking a thumb over his shoulder.

"What the hell?" asked Maisy, not sure what to make of his manner. Everyone else in the pub looked up. Edmund explained that there had been a discovery of treasure at the hall, and it was of considerable size. The coroner's office had just called him as, for some reason, they couldn't get hold of anyone at the Hall. Many glances were exchanged but that didn't work very well so they were quickly swapped back again.

"I don't understand!" hissed Andy, beside himself and his wife. "That place has been on life support since the eighties! How…?"

"They wouldn't tell me any more!" dismissed Edmund, grinning. "But, if this find is as big as it seems, it might turn out that the Hall won't need any financial help from anyone." Maisy hid her grin behind her hands as she rested on them casually.

"There must be some kind of mistake!" sneered Timothy. "If it's been there all this time it either can't be worth all that much, or it doesn't belong to the owner of the property."

"I'm sure all will become clear in time," was Edmund's enigmatic response. Agatha scoffed at that.

Both the Kings and the Williams had convinced themselves that Robin and Olivia would be forced to call on them for help eventually. They'd devoted the entirety of their capricious intellects into working out how to out-muscle the other. The idea that something else might step in to save them had simply never occurred to them. They both agreed the Hall was crucial to the survival of the village, but neither of them were serious about trying to save it. They had taken a look and seen the decline, the quiet and the history. They had completely missed the embers of hope smouldering quietly in the corner. They were not the only ones to make the oversight.

As the pub erupted into conversation, Mick quietly approached Maisy at the bar where she was talking to Edmund.

"Same again," he said. "One for yourselves?"

"I believe it's a little early for me, but as today won't come again …" smiled Edmund.

"You've talked us into it," joked Maisy. While she was busy pouring, Mick asked a question in a low voice.

"Why did they call you? Why not the pub or, frankly, anyone else?" he enquired, shrewdly.

"*God moves in mysterious ways*," he smiled, knowingly. Mick started to laugh and so did Edmund. Maisy glanced up at them, mildly unsettled.

"What's so funny?"

"We were just talking about miracles," said Edmund.

"Yeah, something like that," agreed Mick.

\*

"Wouldn't want to bump into anyone," replied Peter, leading the way through the trees. They were yomping down towards the village after lunch but, as Peter said, it would be best if they remained inconspicuous. Fido was having a grand old time sniffing everything – luckily, he was a dog. They emerged from the woods at the end of a street and immediately adjacent was Kat's cottage. Across the gate a wooden plaque gave the name of the property – Sanctuary Cottage. The garden was neat, if a little small, with well-ordered flowerbeds and a short path leading from the gate to the door.

More flowers were hanging from the walls on either side of the door. A silver bell presented itself, and Peter rang it.

"This is lovely," said Olivia, looking around. "We should have visited before."

Peter frowned and pressed the bell again, before sighing. "Her hearing is not what it once was. I'll go see if she's around the back," he said, moving away. Olivia sighed and casually stepped back and forth between two of the slabs which made up the path.

"I wish we didn't have to avoid the village," she mused, sadly. "It's really very nice here …"

"She's not there. Maybe she went to the Hall and we've missed each other," said Peter, returning swiftly. Robin tried the door, and, to everyone's surprise, it wasn't locked. Had to be the only door in the village that wasn't …

"Kat!" he called as they entered the tiny hallway. Kat's walking stick was there, propped against the coat stand, ready for use. Peter and Robin were first into the lounge and they halted abruptly at the sight of Kat. She was sitting in her armchair, eyes closed, motionless.

"Kat!" repeated Peter. Olivia had a sinking feeling the moment she saw her. Robin and Peter quickly established she wasn't breathing, and she was cold to the touch.

"I'll call an ambulance," she said softly.

# CHAPTER THIRTEEN

Tomlinson Hall

Part Three: Home

Someone being declared dead is, at the same time, deeply profound and mindbogglingly banal. The person who said the words, ran through the process, delivered the ceremony, would be trained to keep their own emotions in check. This was difficult if you struggled with chess. Personally, Robin had never understood the castle move. It was hard enough trying to remember the nuances of each piece, but the second you could move more than one at once, he was at sea! What did death have to do with chess? Well, that would depend on how long the game lasted … If you knew or loved the deceased it would be all encompassing, unforgettably wretched. On the other hand, death is the most common thing in the world, and happens to everyone eventually. Your philosophical bent dictates if that is limiting or liberating.

While they'd not known her very long, Kat had made a big impression on Robin and Olivia. The prime concern for Robin was his own sanity. Natural causes apparently, that bit was all right, even expected. The time of death was what unsettled him – somewhere between 23:00 and 02:00 the previous evening. If that was true, how could he have possibly seen her in the morning? Had he somehow imagined it? The conversation had been exceedingly odd, he recalled. Yet the box with the ring was still in his pocket, thus proving that the interaction had occurred. Right? Unfortunately, this was just the tip of the iceberg and Robin wouldn't have been surprised if it was somehow related to the one with which the Titanic tragically collided.

Although they knew Kat was a nickname, they'd believed that Polly-Ann Smyth was her original name. It turned out they were wrong, and they were shocked when the truth was uncovered. Her real name was Catharine. Catharine Williams. Yes, the same Williams family as Timothy, Sam, Mick and the rest. She had once been their aunt but, due to being Jack Tomlinson's lover, she'd been ostracised by not only Henry and Anne but her own family too, as the rivalry had morphed into Romeo and Juliet proportions.

"Why didn't she tell us?" asked Olivia, confused.

"Because she wanted the Hall to go to you," stated Peter softly. "She feared her identity would complicate matters."

"Did you know?" asked Robin.

"I wanted to tell you, but I gave my word that I would not. She believed that if you were left alone for long enough, you could do what she couldn't. She knew all too well about the tunnels, but she couldn't find the gate key and she knew it would be theft if she took anything – even if it was to pay off the debt. One of the tunnels leads directly into the cellar of her cottage," explained Peter.

"There's more, isn't there, Peter?" asked Olivia, crossing her arms.

"Jack was besotted with Kat and she with him. It was that summer back in 1970 when they really started to get serious. A year later, when Henry and Anne found out about the romance, Henry insisted that Jack ended it. Anne was conflicted but didn't argue with her husband. The Williamses, who hated Henry as much as he did them, basically gave Kat an ultimatum: end it now or we will never speak to you again. She was to be disowned, spurned, forcefully removed, if you will. Love did not conquer all on this occasion, and while Jack pretended to end it to appease his father, Kat refused to deceive her own family. As a result, they kicked her out. She left the village and didn't return until the early eighties when she bought Sanctuary Cottage."

"Henry died in 1973, so why did she stay away for so long?" asked Robin in confusion.

"I see you've been reading that book too," noted Olivia with a smirk. He pulled a face at her and she grinned.

"She tried to rekindle her relationship with Jack but he wasn't the same man as she remembered. He was in the Falklands War, you see. PTSD. He didn't believe she was the same woman," he explained.

"No!" gasped Olivia, horrified. "That's awful!"

"Not to mention Jack's brother, Edward, who did his level best to disrupt her attempts to find love again. He was the one who convinced Jack that if she'd really loved him, she'd never have abandoned him."

"She had no choice. She was thrown out by her own family and couldn't stay with him because of his father," retorted Robin with more passion than he thought he meant.

"Then, after Edward's death, Jack just vanished without a word, and she stayed in the hope he would come back," sighed Peter, looking fraught. "I don't think he ever did." Olivia brushed away a tear.

"She seemed so happy, but I knew there was sadness there," she said, managing to contain her other tears.

"She really loved you two, by the way, she often said to me that she knew you could do it, she knew you could save this place," said Peter. "And Jack ... she couldn't ever forget her Jack. He planned to marry her, you know, way back when."

"Before the war damaged him," murmured Robin in understanding. What Kat had said to him the last time they had spoken was now making a lot more sense. She must have known she was dying somehow! It would explain a lot.

"None of this explains why Jack chose to put us in the will!" groaned Olivia, still at a loss. "I fail to see how he could have known or even heard of either of us."

"Kat didn't know that either, but by that point I think she thought it was Jack's last instruction to her and she clung on just long enough to ensure it would happen," he replied.

"This is so weird," sighed Robin, defeated. "We could have been anybody!"

"But you weren't," Peter reminded him. "Through some chance decision or through brilliance, I believe Jack to have chosen wisely."

"We appreciate that, but not knowing how is a little unnerving," muttered Olivia. "And we still don't know who the fourth beneficiary is!"

"That much was the same for Kat, too. We spent a long time trying to figure out who it could be," stated Peter, pouring more tea.

"I'm convinced it's someone in America, a distant relation," said Olivia. "Kat didn't think so, but she didn't have any better ideas."

"They would have showed up by now," dismissed Robin with a sigh.

"We're assuming they even know what's going on! Besides, something else might have prevented them. Perhaps their instruction is to remain aloof and anonymous until some stage later. Maybe they're in prison or something," she shrugged. "You don't know, they could have been involved in an accident."

"When was the Falklands War?" asked Robin, sharply.

"1982," replied Peter, instantly. "Why?"

"Whenabouts? June?" he asked, starting to flick through the papers.

"It ended in June, I believe," he replied, coming over.

"That's when these payments started coming in, the HRH ones," he said animatedly. "It's related to the war; it's got to be!" Olivia checked on her phone and nodded.

"It would be a huge coincidence if it wasn't related," she concurred.

"He did have a lot of friends from his army days," noted Peter, trying to remember. "Maybe one of them is the fourth beneficiary, but it still wouldn't explain why they aren't here."

"It might if they had different instructions to us," repeated Olivia, exasperated. "Yes … wait!" She darted from the room and furtled through her handbag furiously. Both men watched in abject terror – no man ever knew what fresh hell may emerge from such a place.

"Here," she said, producing a book. It was a diary, an old one from 1982. "Kat found some books and left them for me to read. I might have paid closer attention if I'd known *whose* diary I was being given." Peter laughed and looked up towards the ceiling. Typical Kat! She always preferred to leave clues to lead one to an answer she already knew. It was her way of determining how smart you were.

"Jack's?" guessed Robin as she plonked it down in front of them. The script was fairly easy to read. "There …?"

"May 1$^{st}$ … *My only regret is that I must leave her behind*," read Olivia quickly. "Look at the way this book is folded – she must have pored over this particular page for years!"

"Doesn't say why," muttered Robin.

"We *know* why! Because of the family feuds, that's why!" she almost yelled.

"All right, peace in the valley," he said, raising his hands. She laughed. "And they couldn't run away together because of Edward and the Hall."

"Edward didn't care about this place, only the money it could get him so he could carry on gambling," muttered Peter.

"But …" began Robin before slumping back in his chair. It was all far too late now for any of that. "I wonder where he went," he said, breathing out heavily.

"France," Olivia offered with a shrug. "America? Anywhere but here, I suspect. Of course, in those days it was way easier to just disappear."

Peter shuddered and they looked up at him in anxiety.

"Sorry, you're talking about the eighties as if it's ancient history. I shall feel better soon," he sighed forlornly.

"So … if Kat was Catharine Williams, does that mean the funeral will be held here?" asked Olivia.

"Actually, no, she has many friends in other places and I doubt she will be buried here. Truth was, she loved the Hall, tolerated the village, and ignored mostly everyone who lived here," replied Peter. "Edmund and I are the obvious exceptions."

"Edmund! He knows about one of the tunnels leading from the pub to the church! He and Maisy use it as a secret meeting place," Olivia said.

"You think Maisy is the fourth beneficiary?" asked Robin.

"Well … we're total strangers to him, and so would she be, so it makes sense," she shrugged. "Obviously we now know they aren't strangers at all, but maybe Jack didn't."

"*As far as we know*. It could also be Edmund himself; he said he was following instructions he was given, remember?"

"Without context, that could have been about anything," she argued. "They were discussing secrets, one of which is clearly their relationship."

"The vicar and the landlady – sounds like some kind of play," remarked Peter, with a little nod. "*I'd* go and see it."

"We don't know what their secrets are, and they have known

about that passageway for ages, though they might not even know it connects with the Hall – the gate was locked, after all," she persisted.

"If you were to approach Edmund and give him the impression you already knew, you might trick him into revealing more," suggested Peter astutely. "You could try and appeal to his sense of honesty. As a man of the Church, it would be difficult for him to resist that."

"What about Mick, the farmer? He's been one step ahead of this from the rest of the village," asked Robin.

"He's a Williams, a black sheep I grant you, but still a Williams," replied Peter, shrugging.

"The only way to discover more is to confront them; we'll get nowhere guessing," sighed Olivia. "We can visit Edmund and pretend we want to enquire about Kat's funeral."

It was early evening by the time they set off, Fido tugging on the lead as usual. The sun was going down – well, strictly speaking, the earth was rotating, thus giving the impression of the sun going down.

"I really love this place," said Olivia, sighing. "Feels more like home than anywhere else."

"It's nice," he agreed. She was right, they'd never been happy in London.

"Much better than London," she announced. "I mean, London's cool and everything, but it doesn't have what this place does."

"Charm? Lack of congestion charges …?"

"Green soul," she smiled, waving a hand up at the trees overhead.

"As long as you promise never to turn into a hippy pagan or anything," he grinned. "And if you insist on talking to the plants, please don't do it in front of anyone."

The church's stained-glass windows gently glowed in a range colours as they approached, filtering and intensifying the delicate candlelight like a spiritual beacon. Such effort, passion, and diligence in each tiny pane, painting perpendicular pictures of biblical significance for all to see. It did look very beautiful but, inwardly at any rate, they prepared for an awkward conversation. They made their way down the path towards the doors and then into the church itself. Organ music gently played but they could hear music of another kind from a room further inside. The sign outside stated it was band practice night.

Robin noticed a tiny golden plaque on the wall, among many others. It read: *We judge by appearance, unlike God who judges everything.* It reminded Robin about a stimulating, semi-pseudo-intellectual chat he and Arni had had one night nearly a year ago. Arni had asked him what he thought preceded consciousness. Robin still had no answer to that beyond subconsciousness.

Olivia tugged his arm. "Stop putting it off," she growled, knowing he was delaying on purpose.

"I'm not stopping you…" he grinned.

"I'm not doing it by myself," she said, stubbornly.

As if on cue, Edmund emerged from the room, carrying a guitar. One of the strings was trailing after him and he was probably going to get a new one so he could re-string the instrument. Olivia cleared her throat to get his attention and he looked up before smiling.

"Hello!" he said, in a pantomime whisper. "I'll be with you in two shakes."

"Ready?" asked Robin. Olivia nodded. Having apparently given up trying to find the string, Edmund carefully propped the instrument up on a chair before coming over to them.

"Hello again," he said, as he got close. "I am sorry for your loss."

"You knew her far longer than we did, Reverend," Olivia reminded him, sadly. "You don't need to feel sorry for us; we should feel sorry for you and the village." An expression flashed across his face but instead of addressing what the village really thought of Kat, he just smiled and nodded his head.

"So, just three of us left," remarked Robin, deciding to go for it. Truth was, he just hated awkward silences. Edmund tilted his head a little.

"Yup," nodded Olivia. "We can handle it now though, I think."

"Grief is always an individual's journey as much as it is a family's or even a nation's …" began Edmund, artfully.

"We know about the tunnels, and we know you know," stated Olivia, firmly. She was very careful not to sound aggressive. Indeed, she sounded quite congenial. "Just like we know Maisy knows too."

There was a long pause. "Ah…" he settled on, finally. He pulled a face and motioned for them to follow him into one of the side rooms where the tea and mugs were located.

"Tea?" he asked, clearly caught out. "Or would you prefer coffee?"

"Tea, please," she said, easily.

"Why didn't you say something? We may have found the treasure far sooner, had we known," Robin wanted to know.

"Because, in my codicil, I was told I couldn't tell you anything," he admitted, pouring the tea. He closed his eyes and breathed in the steam before sighing and pouring two more. He sat across from them. He was relieved the truth, or at least most of it, was now out in the open.

"That's why I kept having to hint that more would be found at the Hall. I knew something had to be there because of the tunnel. Jack Tomlinson was a complicated man. As one of the four oldest families, myself a Clapton, I must admit I did not expect him to seek out my help. Perhaps he did after the way we handled his brother. I know he and my father were friends but I didn't interact with him all that often. I know he had his struggles after the war and, though no one talks about it, he and Kat were once very close."

"We know," stated Robin, plonking the diary on the table in front of him. Edmund slowly reached out his hand.

"May I?" he asked, interested. Olivia nodded. Edmund flicked through the diary and, like everyone else had, landed on the right page.

"Complicated," he sighed, at last. He replaced the diary on the table and took a sip of tea. "Is the Hall safe now?"

"We don't know," said Robin. Then he smiled. "There's a good chance it is."

"That's what Jack would have wanted, I think," he replied. "Anything to keep it away from the Williamses and the Kings. I would like to visit one day, with your permission?"

"Just come by anytime," replied Olivia.

"We used to play in the gardens and woods sometimes, as children. The Hall itself I always found very grand and not a little forbidding. I remember once creeping up those stairs and all those portraits piercing me with their eyes," he recalled with a chuckle.

"So, you and Maisy?" asked Olivia, changing the subject.

"Ah," he said, again. "Yes, I'd be very grateful if you didn't tell anyone about it. We've been seeing each other for years, but I don't think the rest of the village would appreciate the secrecy."

"Not a word," responded Robin, making a zipping gesture across his mouth.

"Thank you."

"The only thing we don't know now is, why us?" sighed Olivia. "I had hoped you might know."

"The only hint I received was that he trusted Robin because he was the son of a friend of a friend of his. See … you haven't read all of this diary yet, have you?"

"We have been rather preoccupied," smiled Olivia. "You know, exploring abandoned tunnels and trying to figure out who the other benefactor was."

"May I?" he asked, rather pointlessly. Again, he flicked through the book, in the general area of the page everyone had read. He frowned as he found what he was looking for and calmly replaced his tea on the pad.

"Either of you know anyone called Primrose?" he asked.

# CHAPTER FOURTEEN

# Primrose would have been proud

It was very dark by the time Robin and Olivia were led outside the church by Fido. Evensong was winding down, the birds were quietening, and what little light there was left was fading. So just to be clear, it was certainly not high noon. The sun no longer had his hat on; indeed, he was crawling around on the floor looking for it. Would he ever find it again?

In silence, they followed the path through the graveyard and paused to look upon the Tomlinson graves. The looked no different than they had before, yet somehow they felt different. It wasn't exactly that there had been an undercurrent of tension or restlessness before, not in any tangible sense. That said, there seemed a certain satisfaction in the air. A sense that things had been put to rest, if a little strangely.

Strolling out onto the road in front of the pub, they didn't even glance in its direction. Instead, they sauntered up the road back towards the Hall.

"Peter will have retired to his cottage by now, fear of the Hall in the dark," remarked Robin, in a half-hearted attempt at humour.

"I'm not sure it's a thing anymore, not now that we're the lord and lady of the manor," she replied.

"Shall we be one of those annoying couples that redesign the whole thing and offend the entire village?"

"We may have already managed that," she giggled. "Most of it, certainly."

They went quiet again and heard an owl somewhere off in the distance.

"Are we going to stay here, do you think?" he asked, softly.

"Yes, I think we will."

It was a great place, somewhere they couldn't ever have realistically acquired any other way. After all the dreams, the madness, and the intrigue, it somehow felt right. If someone had asked him, a year ago, how would his life turn out, this wouldn't have been his answer. If that same someone had asked him a year later about what his opinion would have been the year before, he wouldn't have answered at all.

"So, Primrose was the link all along," she sighed, shaking her head. "And there was me digging like an idiot in Virginia."

"I wonder what happened and who the third person was," he replied.

"Whoever it was, had to have been connected to the royal family in a pretty major way for the Queen to repay them like that. Primrose never said anything?"

"No, course not. I was just a child when he died. Hardly the sort of audience for that kind of story. Besides, maybe my dad didn't want him to. I mean, they were close. I'm surprised he never mentioned anything."

"You were at Primrose's funeral and there was no talk of any of this then … maybe Jack Tomlinson somehow worked it out after he passed," she suggested. "I don't think we're ever going to know for sure."

"No, not now that they're all brown bread," he said, sadly. "The story goes like this. Primrose and Jack Tomlinson were best pals for nearly two years. During the Falklands conflict they were somehow instrumental in the result, in a way that compelled the royal family to personally compensate them. Those regular payments are now coming from King Charles and, assuming they were paying Primrose too, that would have stopped when he died. Jack used the fund to stay ahead of the interest payments of the debt his brother incurred and … and we know the rest."

"I wonder what they did," she groaned, annoyed at not having the complete picture.

"Whatever it was, it must have been pretty epic," he shrugged. "Official Secrets Act prohibits any further disclosure – that's what was said, anyway."

"It does sort of explain the peculiar choices for beneficiaries. He chose us because of Primrose, Kat because they were lovers, and the vicar due to his friendship with his father," she listed. "He must have valued Primrose a lot."

"Only as much as Primrose valued me, apparently," he shrugged. Then he grinned and pulled her closer. "You just got lucky." She laughed.

"Yeah, I got lucky! We're both lucky that my dad knew what to do!" He agreed that that was undeniable. The mention of her father reminded him of something else, too. The ring was still in its box; he hadn't yet found time to ask her. He had to do it! But when was the best time? What if she said no? What if she didn't hear the question properly? Many a pub quiz had been lost due to tragic misunderstandings such as those.

"Babe, do you mind if I ask you something?" he asked, floundering inwardly.

"Of course not," she answered, unconcerned.

"If someone wanted to ask someone else a question but was worried about the answer, what would be the best way to ask it?" he asked, hating himself.

"Who?" she asked immediately.

"Just someone …" he trailed off.

"Yeah, but it would depend on who was asking who about what."

"What?"

"Person A and person B," she replied as they reached the driveway.

"Just hypothetically," he specified unhelpfully, losing patience with himself.

"So, hypothetically … person A wants to ask person B a question, but we don't know who either of them are or what the question is supposed to be?" was her sceptical response. "And you want to know how to word the question for the best?"

"In a nutshell," he nodded, realising how stupid that sounded.

"A coconut, maybe …" she muttered, frowning. "Is this one of those weird 'how to tell if you're a psychopath' questions?"

"The question I'm asking you, or the question they're asking each other?"

"They can't both ask the same question, surely?"

"Who?"

"Whoever these hypothetical people are!" she yelled, with a laugh. Fido barked, as if laughing too. Yes, that was a lousy attempt if even the dog found it funny.

"Ok, let's start again," he said, decisively. "If you knew someone who …"

"Will you just …! What are you trying to say?" she cut in, exasperated.

"Oh … it was just a joke," he sighed, giving up.

"About what?" she questioned, confused.

"I didn't tell it right; it's about metaphysics," he bluffed.

"Metaphysics … right," she said, mulling it over. She remembered something from a while ago when he'd done something similar.

"Do we have to pretend to be person A and person B?" she asked, suspiciously.

"What? It doesn't matter," he brushed her off. "Forget I even mentioned it." They entered the Hall and Robin locked the door as Fido headed off to his bed, leaving a trail of water droplets from his bowl. Olivia turned the lights on and stretched. They both looked up at the silent staircase and the portraits on the wall. Robin wasn't sure why, but he imagined their question to him would be: did you ask her yet? It was as if the whole Hall was holding its breath. He was trying, he was really trying, but this was a lot trickier than he'd first envisaged. Just four words – little ones too – nothing complicated. He had the ring – arguably they had the money – there were no awkward family complications. What was the difficulty?

"Do you want dinner?" she asked, breaking him out of his thoughts. A different set of four words, but still a question! Was that a sign from the universe? Not that he needed another one.

"What if you didn't?" he blurted, as if it was crucial.

"Then I wouldn't make myself any," she answered, puzzled. They stared at one another for a second.

"Robin, what is wrong with you?" she asked. "Aren't you hungry?"

"Yes, yes I am," he replied, trying to organise his thoughts.

"Then you do want dinner?"

"Yes, but if you didn't want to, you'd say, wouldn't you?" he asked, clearly talking about something else.

She smiled and advanced towards him.

"Robin … there are times in our relationship when we have problems talking to one another. I don't mean communication hiatuses, arguments, or misunderstandings. I mean, literally times when what comes out of your mouth might as well be a different language. This is clearly one of those times. Now, I know something is bothering you, but you don't seem able to articulate what it is. Now, I'm no psychologist, but I know when it comes to you that if it's not bed or food then it's in your head. So … you leave me no choice … if you don't say what you really want to say, I'm going to turn around, walk away, and then go to bed without making us any food. Do I make myself clear?"

"Steady on," he laughed, nervously.

"Please," she pleaded, hugging him. "Just say it."

"I don't want you to say no," he admitted, awkwardly.

"I'll probably say yes," she replied, trying not to sound too impatient.

"Can we …?" he began.

"What? What do you want?"

"Can we go upstairs to the library?" he finally said, still hating himself. She scowled up at him.

"Fine," she growled, leading the way.

They walked up the stairs together, rather slowly. Robin glanced at the portraits on the way up, hoping to see some encouragement from them. Instead, he saw the usual dour and disinterested expressions. He took a fleeting look over his shoulder and saw what might have been Kat standing at the bottom of the stairs. She was gone after he blinked in surprise. Great! More hallucinations! This was meant to be a happy occasion and all he was doing was infuriating Olivia and wounding his own mind.

The moment they entered the library, Robin clapped his eyes on the sword again. Suddenly, though he might never know why, he felt a lot braver. They stopped right in front of the cabinet, and he stared down into Olivia's eyes. She stared back, bewilderment and what might have been hope on her sweet face. This was it, this was the moment that perhaps his whole life had been building towards.

Robin, still holding her hands, began to kneel before her as apparently was the traditional way of things. Let's just hope there wasn't a sudden attack of cramp. Her eyes went wide, but she didn't say anything. Letting go of one of her hands, he fished in his pocket for the ring and quickly found it. Phew! Wouldn't want that to go walkies at a time like this.

"Olivia Higgins …" he began.

"What? Why are you talking like that?" she almost shrieked.

"Will you marry me?" he asked with surprising ease. Her mouth opened; he just spotted her eyes starting to roll back and leapt up to catch her as she fainted.

"Wow," he breathed, heaving her into a chair. "I was really worrying about the wrong things."

Turned out there was nothing in the book about what to do if the woman faints during your proposal – and those comments on Reddit were not helpful. You know who you are, I tried it and things are worse now.

Olivia awoke with a jerk – unfortunate phrase.

"Yes!" she breathed, grinning. "I don't know what happened there … I just went."

"That's great. Do we need to get a doctor or something?" he asked.

"Are you crazy?" she giggled, wrapping her arms around him. "I've never felt this good! Do you know how long I have waited for you to ask me that?"

"Err, no," he said, between kisses.

"Ages!"

"You could have asked me to marry you," he reminded her. "I thought you hated gender stereotypes."

"I've never really been technically minded; you had to help me set up my Apple music," she jested.

"Seriously, though, you could have asked. I wouldn't have minded. Actually, it would have been much less nerve racking for me."

"I did think of that, but I couldn't decide what ring I wanted," she admitted, sadly. "Wait ..." She examined the ring more closely. "This ... isn't this ...?" Instantly he knew what she meant.

They hurried to the portrait on the stairs. Suzanna Tomlinson regarded them as she always did, though Robin could swear she looked happier. They compared their ring to the one on her finger in the portrait, and concluded it was the same one. The Tomlinson ring. As they prepared dinner, Robin told her all about the conversation he'd had with Kat and that she'd passed it on to him.

"Crazy," concluded Olivia, staring at the ring on her finger. "But surely ... wasn't she already dead then?"

"I don't know, I'm trying not to think about that part," he replied. She shook her head but smiled.

"Well, dead or alive, she got us right."

"I think ... I think she didn't want us to go the same way that she and Jack did," he explained.

"I can see why – that was heart-breaking," responded Olivia. "What would you have done if I'd said no?"

"I'd have felt very foolish." She laughed. "I was pretty sure you'd say yes though," he smiled, pulling her into another hug. "You're always polite."

"I'd have said anything for food," she jested. Then she became serious. "In our lives we're told never to make quick decisions. There's a modus operandi, we weigh the pros and cons, consult institutions, friends, and family before we make a move. Then sometimes … it feels right to do the opposite."

"Spontaneity?" he offered.

"It's more than that, it's freedom."

"Freedom to make our own mistakes," he nodded.

"I've made worse mistakes than you," she grinned. "I can just imagine you on the phone with Citizens Advice. 'Hello, my name is Robin, should I marry the best woman in the world?'"

"Hey, who's to say you've peaked? Plenty of room for more mistakes. The friendly illusion we know as time is never present," he laughed.

"To mark this special occasion," she began, quickly updating her calendar to plan future anniversaries, "how about we cook homemade lasagne?" He hesitated and she laughed. "I swear I won't mess it up this time. With a kitchen this size it will be so much easier to manage."

"If you're sure, I'm in," he answered.

Over the next few days, they spread the news of their engagement to their families and close friends. Overall, it was received warmly but without much surprise. Indeed, a few who had not been so in touch over the years expressed astonishment that they were not already married. They planned the wedding to some degree, deciding to hold the party at the Hall. This was made easy by Peter volunteering to take care of the catering. When the villagers discovered the news, their reaction, too, was positive. Many were secretly hopeful that a new owner and fortune might save the village. Even those who'd wanted the Hall for themselves begrudgingly admitted that it was better in the Meadows' hands than no hands at all.

Sadly, many other villages would vanish over time, relegated to the history they were always destined for. Albany-on-Lea, however, was set for a second chance. Robin and Olivia had quickly decided to remain in the Hall. Olivia could continue with her career, whereas Robin decided not to bother with the rat race anymore. London had taught him a lot, he would always say, but it was not where his heart was. Besides, some of those rats could be quite vicious when cornered. As a present, the Mayor of Chipping Barnet wanted to commission a portrait of them to add to those of the Tomlinsons on the staircase.

The destination for the honeymoon proved the most difficult. Olivia wanted to go to Paris but Robin preferred Milan or Barcelona. It was Peter who, to end the increasingly hostile debate, suggested Stanley. His opinion was that it would be more meaningful to their new home and, most likely, cheaper. It would also be easier to bring Fido and accommodate him there – both Robin and Olivia had used Fido as an excuse to get out of deciding at various stages in the argument. There was also the point of it, Stanley that is, being an unusual destination too. While they were sure that they couldn't be the only couple to honeymoon on the island, the place wasn't exactly a top ten choice.

One night, as he was closing the curtains, Robin thought he saw something very strange: a man and a woman standing in the centre of the Hall's driveway. The man looked a lot like a young version of Robert Plant, with long wavy hair, denim waistcoat and a silver medallion. The woman next to him was radiantly beautiful, had long brown hair and wore a long purple and blue dress. He blinked and they were gone. Had he just seen the ghosts of Jack and Catharine as they would have looked in 1970? Before the family feuds, the financial calamity, and the Falkland war took their toll? Robin still did not believe in ghosts and hoped his mind was just recalibrating or something.

"Do you think the Meadows will last as long here as the Tomlinsons?" asked Olivia later in bed.

"Not if we aren't careful," he chuckled.

"It would be really cool to be part of a dynasty," she noted.

"Is that a subtle way of asking me if we should have kids?" he enquired, turning out the light.

"No!" she giggled. "I mean, I didn't know you could feel history."

"What?"

"That's not the right word, is it?"

"I don't know, I'm not sure I know what you mean," he said.

"I've said it before, but this place just feels right," she concluded after a sleepy sigh. "Like we've been here forever, and we will be here forever because it's where we're supposed to be." A very fake sounding snore came from Robin, and she booted him in the shin, earning a surprised groan.

In each other's arms they drifted off to sleep, finally at ease in their new home. To be fair, it did say so on the painted glass: *Home sweet home, where the hearts are, where it is good to be.* It *was* a good place, a solid refuge unbowed by the ravages of time and controversy. The grandfather clock ticked loudly, making one of Fido's ears twitch occasionally. Even the ghosts slid into slumber, perhaps sated by the knowledge that their legacy was safe. Or maybe just exhausted, like everyone else – who knows?

# CHAPTER FIFTEEN

# The Ninth from 1970

It was too late; the bedroom door was open, and all the desperate pretences shattered.

Fido was bounding for the mail after hearing the postman coming a mile away. This postman always made a funny shrieking sound when Fido was around and, like many dogs, Fido loved to make an impression. Sadly, however, he heard the footsteps tearing away down the driveway as the chap, experienced now, beat a hasty retreat. Doubling back in the forest, he then zigzagged back to his van.

"Don't you dare eat those letters, Fido!" called Olivia as she regally descended the stairs towards the hall. Fido stood over them, panting heavily, his slobber ready to drip.

"Good boy," she said, scooping them off the doormat adeptly.

"If you like, I can get one of those metal mail holders," offered Peter, shears in hand as he attempted to bring order back to the garden.

"No, it's fine, he's much better now," she grinned. "*Darling!*" she yelled, making Peter jump.

"Breakfast!"

A muffled cry from Robin, who was upstairs, was heard. "Well, hurry up or I'll give it to Fido." Fido barked, always hopeful for extras.

"Coming!" yelled Robin. Olivia smiled as she tracked his footsteps across the upstairs floor, down the stairs and into the room.

"You wouldn't really give my breakfast away, would you?" he demanded, amused.

"Of course not," she replied. She then mouthed to Fido. "I totally would."

"So, I checked it out and I think the village will be in favour of doing the annual fate," Robin said, continuing on from their discussion the previous evening. He eyed Fido suspiciously. Olivia began to tie his tie properly, as he had apparently lost that ability. The fog of morning, he called it. Laziness was what she called it – it had many names.

"Where is it going to be held?"

"That's the funny thing, nowhere does it actually specify," he replied, trying to remember. "I think the village green, but it doesn't seem big enough somehow."

"Won't the war memorial get in the way?" she queried. Robin shrugged. "Edmund will know, won't he? I mean …" She lowered her voice. "He was alive when they held the last one, right?"

Robin chuckled.

"I'll think of a tactful way to ask him," he responded, easily. He began buttering her toast, what a filthy thing to do. He heard her tearing at envelopes and rustling around in the recycling when it all went silent. He turned to see her reading something intently.

"You're not going to …" she began, stunned.

"What?" he asked, worried. She pushed her glasses up her nose as if to see better.

"It's another one of those codicil things!" she growled, bringing it over.

"Oh no," he grunted, hoping she was joking. Such hopes were dashed as he too began to read it.

*My dears, if you are reading this then I'm probably not with you anymore. I should hope so, anyway, otherwise it means there's been an appalling error somewhere. I know we didn't know each other a long time but you both proved to be very good friends and a much-needed comfort. I wish you both nothing but the best. Now, here's the tricky part. It's complicated but the short story is, I own some property and I would like you two to help sort things out. The details are here …*

"I don't want to worry you but it says codicil nine … that implies to me there are eight others," Robin said in a low voice.

A few hours later, Robin, Olivia and Fido were back on the M25. They found their way to a small village and drove past a little church where a funeral was taking place. Just outside the village they drove down a long, windy driveway towards a large manor. Binglesham House was as uninviting and bleak as it was possible to be without being outright hostile. Slowly, they got out of the car as a family unhurriedly emerged to regard them from the entrance.

"Here we go again," said Olivia, attaching Fido's lead.

"At least we didn't get the storm this time," he began, just as thunder rolled in the distance.

"That's done it, well done," she said with a mischievous grin. "I'm just relieved you didn't say anything about getting lost."

Far above, in a dimly lit window, a figure stared down at the new arrivals on the driveway. As the rain began to fall and lightning flickered in the distance, Binglesham House mourned the death of its long-time owner, Polly-Ann Smyth …

# EPILOGUE

Hold the mirror up to your face. What do you see? You never see the same person, not really. Every second brings change, even to the individual. Nothing is constant, everything comes to an end. It's because of how fragile and ephemeral things are that we cherish them so. What do you see? You'll always see the reflection, or you'll turn into stone. You are Medusa and you are Perseus, both together. The one thing the mirror can always show is your past; it can never show your potential. Don't give up, even if you lose your thread in the labyrinth of life, and always remember that the Minotaur, figurative of course, is lost too.

Did Robin and Olivia escape the cycle of neverendingly ending up in other people's wills? Could Fido ever get over his craving for fresh post? And what did happen in the Falklands war that contributed so much to this strange story?

Sometimes, the most frustrating thing in life is when there are no answers, there is no closure. Who am I? Is God real? Blah, blah … Just in case you needed any examples. At the time of writing this, it's impossible to know if these answers can be found. Currently, the best estimations I can give are yes, no and I don't know. Makes it sound like multiple choice, I know, but isn't that a lot like life? Multiple choices. Just long lines of choices and paths to follow. The truth is, I don't know what happens next for any of it. I wish them both the very best. They were both very dear friends of mine. Who am I?

Have you not guessed yet? Yes, that's right, it is me, Catharine Williams. You don't know me, you never will either. You're the tenth codicil. There is something in your life you need to do … please get on with it, it's later than you think.

# AFTERWORD

It all ended at the end. Or did it? Some people would say nothing ever ends as it never truly started. Not to worry though, those people are usually recaptured within twenty business days. The afterword is defined as a literary device (they're not wrong, it's even got the word 'word' in it) usually placed at the conclusion of a piece of work (this is some piece of work). It's often about where the idea for the work came from, or how the book was written. I shall honour this tradition.

This book was written on a device called a laptop. A laptop is a battery-powered computer, whereas a computer is an electrical device (that word again) for processing or storing data. The idea, or I should say the divine notion for this, came to me from the netherworld of thought and consciousness, and can I just say how thankful I am to be a part of that world? The answer is yes, I can indeed ask. So, if anyone reading this has got anything out of any of this, you're the first. Congratulations, you must be very proud.

# APPENDICES

Appendix A: *Chronicles of Barnet – Legacy of the Tomlinsons* – Professor of History Tracey Stannett MSc

Appendix B: *The Diary of Jack Tomlinson 1982* – Jack Tomlinson

### BY THE SAME AUTHOR ALSO AVAILABLE ON AMAZON:

OPERATION HERETIC (THE OBSENNETH SERIES Book 9)

OPERATION TERMINUS (THE OBSENNETH SERIES Book 8)

OPERATION EPICENTRE (THE OBSENNETH SERIES Book 7)

OPERATION NOMAD (THE OBSENNETH SERIES Book 6)

OPERATION NIGHTSHADE (THE OBSENNETH SERIES Book 5)

OPERATION EMERALD (THE OBSENNETH SERIES Book 4)

OPERATION SELECTOR (THE OBSENNETH SERIES Book 3)

OPERATION BLACKLIGHT (THE OBSENNETH SERIES Book 2)

OPERATION ORION (THE OBSENNETH SERIES Book 1)